Omnisc

By
S.E. Raftery

Dear Joe,

thank you for your support !

Love from Serena xxx

MAPLE
PUBLISHERS

Omniscient

Author: S.E. Raftery

Copyright © S.E. Raftery (2023)

The right of S.E. Raftery to be identified as author of this work has been asserted by the author in accordance with section 77 and 78 of the Copyright, Designs and Patents Act 1988.

First Published in 2023

ISBN 978-1-915796-83-7 (Paperback)
978-1-915796-84-4 (Hardback)
978-1-915796-85-1 (Ebook)

Book cover design and Book layout by:
White Magic Studios
www.whitemagicstudios.co.uk

Published by:
Maple Publishers
Fairbourne Drive, Atterbury,
Milton Keynes,
MK10 9RG, UK
www.maplepublishers.com

A CIP catalogue record for this title is available from the British Library.

In Loving Memory of Patrick John Raftery
And
Peter Charles Raftery

During war and strife,

The anxieties of life,

Calathea is a place,

To take your space,

Clear your mind,

Leave your stress behind.

I created Calathea at a time in my life that I found the world we live in to be very heavy, unforgiving and filled with artificial stressors that we as a species have created. Calathea is a place lacking in technological influence, where one's only responsibility is to have a care for those around them, and enjoy the magnificent space they have been blessed with. There, life is more than traffic jams, deadlines, trying to fit into a 'status quo'. It is simply, life.

Contents

Chapter 1 - The Land of New Beginnings

Anad peered down at the universe below, catching sight of the transparent shadows circling the Earth, observing its inhabitants.

Observing you.

They see everything. Your desires. Your wishes. Your fears. Your secrets.

They see *you*.

It's very lonely up there, despite the collection of spirits hovering in outer space, together in their isolation.

They are the Omniscient spirits- all seeing, all knowing. They are reserved in outer space until selected by the supreme presence, Anad, to take a physical form and walk the Earth alongside the species of the era. A divine being, sent to aid the restoration of harmony, should it be disturbed.

Anad decided that all species that would ever walk the Earth would require the influence of 4 virtues to exist peacefully: unity, abundance, empathy and compromise. Each Omniscient was created to embody one of these virtues, which would influence them to act according to the characteristic of it.

The Omniscients have existed since the dawning of the Earth, and observed every species that has ever inhabited the planet; none gifted with such intelligence and plagued by such selfishness as humanity. The crimes of the Earth, all committed by mankind, a species so bold as to intentionally outwit mother nature. For how long, they wondered...

They continued to drift in familiar solitude, when an unusual feeling swept over them all, and the dark, empty plain that they occupied was replaced by a blinding light. In a dazzling explosion, the Omniscient souls collided for the first time. In a flash of chaos and inexplicable design, their own beautiful story commenced its transcription...

A hurricane of creation formed around the united transparent shadows. The space they occupied began to cave in on itself, and a bright, white light formed in the centre of the cavity, beginning to turn anti-clockwise in a steady motion, quickly ascending in speed. Living, breathing life began to take form in the centre of the chaos. The shadowy mist that encapsulated their souls for as long as they have existed, exploded into an enormous, glittering cloud of miniscule pebbles. The remnants came to an abrupt halt before they reached the edge of the illuminated cavity, and smashed back together to form a heart, beating furiously, glowing gold.

The glow of the golden heart bled into the edges of the cavity, and a soft, ivory cloud emerged, encasing the precious commodity as it spun at a sickening pace around it. The ivory cloud formed the flesh of the Omniscient of Unity, Azriel. In seconds, he stood as the centre of the universe taking shape around him. He touched down gently on the hard ground running across the expanding plain of space.

Before his very eyes, a formation of glorious territory unravelled. Green fields rolling out to the left, trees shooting out of the ground, blossom leaves floating to the ground delicately. A rocky mountain range rose from the ground and water spilled from the sharp drop to form an enormous, crystal-clear waterfall. The body of water travelled across the ground that formed just in time for the water to flow across it, resembling a river that ran all the way from the source, through the valleys.

A sandy tornado raged across the empty land, until the river reached a steep decline and spilled in all directions to cover the sandy floor filled with colourful reef, dry seaweed and moss-covered rocks. Soon, the water had reached the top of the sandy drop, and engulfed the beach for a few metres inland. The waves gently lapped at the shore, glistening under the beam of the sun.

The tornado of sand continued across the beach to the edge of the sea defined by chalky cliffs, extending so far as to form a dry desert. Tumble weeds rolled along lazily, carried by the gentle, arid breeze. Camels padded across the sand, dolphins rose from the water and splashed back into the depths and majestic birds soared across the sky.

The tornado made for the edge of the sea, and a foamy wave crashed against it, throwing it into mid-air to connect with a cumulous cloud that rained down on the water. As it travelled further from the shore, it evolved into a blizzard of blinding white snow, creating towering ice bergs miles out to sea, with mischievous penguins, contentedly sliding on the ice and diving into the water, enticed by the fish leaping from the surface of the water into the air before splashing back into the icy sea. Some fish were not so fortunate as to escape the agile jaws of the seals stalking them from the ice, and the polar bears hunting food for their young.

The water surged away from the icebergs and crashed into a wall of trees to link the ecosystems together and resemble a wide river bordering the forest of trees, buzzing with insects, echoing with the screech of the monkeys and roar of the tigers.

Elephants trumpeting, birds tweeting, horses snorting-it was a sensory overload for Azriel, accustomed to the dark and quiet of space, now faced with all of the creatures he had observed on Earth, but never so freely. The loneliness that consumed him, and the darkness that encapsulated his soul dissipated into an unfamiliar feeling of joy and anticipation.

Breathless, he held out his hands and examined them carefully, the unique grooves in the skin of his fingertips and freckly knuckles.

He began to walk, unsteadily for a while, casting his eyes over the breathtaking beauty of his surroundings. In his peripheral vision, he spotted a tall, muscular, brilliant-white creature galloping across the sand, tracing the lapping water. His long, glossy mane tossed by the wind generated by his sheer speed. The horse noticed Azriel, and immediately changed direction to approach him. Just metres from where he stood, the horse ground to an abrupt halt. The stallion's genuine blue eyes sparkled in the sunshine as he fixed his gaze on Azriel. His tail brushed the floor as he invitingly turned to the side, gesturing for Azriel to climb to his back.

He paused for a moment, before hopping aboard the horse's rigid frame. Before he had found his balance, the horse surged from a standstill to a thrilling gallop, gliding across the soft ground, gathering speed as the wind whipped the man's freckled face.

The horse navigated the deserted plain knowingly, seeming to have a particular destination. His speed descended as they approached a large, wooden structure encased by giant, green leaves, with an entrance decorated by hanging vines, blowing gently in the breeze. He came to a halt once more, and lowered his head, encouraging Azriel to dismount. He swung his leg over the horse's hindquarters and lowered himself to the ground. Not a moment later, Azriel's new companion turned to gallop back toward the sea, and as he met the sea front, a staircase of clouds began to form, and he climbed high into the blue sky, out of sight.

Azriel stood, perplexed, gazing about his surroundings.

Eventually, he decided to investigate the structure standing before him, brushed the hanging vines aside, and entered the cavern. Inside, he found a slow-moving waterfall, which appeared to be suspended in mid-air; the water dissolving to mist before it hit the ground. Curious, he moved closer to the unusual feature, and glanced upwards to find that it led back to the vacuum of space he once occupied. He reached out his hand to touch the clear water, only to be thrust back into the darkness above, where he has languished since the beginning of time. Before the familiar feeling of emptiness had time to creep back into his soul, he plunged his hand back into the blur of light and returned to his position opposite the misty waterfall.

As he stared into the water, he noticed the reflection staring back at him- dazzling blue eyes with turquoise inflections around the circumference, a razor-sharp jaw line and a tanned, freckled face, framed by dark blonde curls. His gaze deviated to his muscular arms, washboard torso and burly legs with sand-coloured, knee-length shorts clinging to them.

'Azriel?' a soft, inquisitive voice filled the cavern in which he thought he stood alone. He turned to see an olive-skinned beauty approaching him. Her deep, brown eyes fixed on him, her plump lips pursed, and silky black hair cascading down her back, swaying gently in the warm breeze.

'Althea.' His pupils dilated as he scanned the beautiful woman stood before him. 'Omniscient of Compromise.'

Slowly, he walked toward her, pausing a metre or so from where she was. They observed one another for a few moments, in awe and bewilderment. Azriel then peeled back the draping vines, and waited for Althea to cross the passage, before following her toward the glittering water, in a comfortable silence.

They ambled the deserted splendour, and the sight that met their eyes was one that they could never have imagined to be in their immediate vicinity, only ever permitted to observe, never to experience as their true selves. They dared not even blink, for fear that it may all be seized from their grasp in a split second, and they'd be returned to the darkness.

'It's very impressive, isn't it?' Azriel asked, sure that she would agree.

'It's *magnificent!*' Althea gasped, staring about her awe-inspiring surroundings. 'But I don't understand, what is this? Why are we here?'

'I can only guess that the collision of our divine souls has created land equipped to satisfy our desires and attributes.'

'And what are your desires, Azriel?' Althea turned to him, a mischievous and seductive glint in her eye.

A smile corrupted Azriel's neutral countenance as he considered Althea's question. He distracted himself by wading into the pleasantly warm ocean. Vibrantly coloured fish darted about the water around them, and tropical birds soared across the brilliant blue sky. Above their heads, they saw the horse that led Azriel to Althea, galloping freely in the clouds.

'Do you think this has ever happened before?' She inquired, suddenly looking serious.

'It hasn't. Omniscient spirits have only ever populated bodies on existing planets, as directed by Anad. They have never created planets of their own.'

'Are we the only people here?' She asked.

'I don't know. I thought I was the only person here, but I was evidently wrong.' Azriel replied, gesturing toward her.

'Shall we go and find out?' She smiled, took his hand in hers and led him back towards the shore.

They journeyed across the land, uncovering its infinite beauty. An aquarium to the right, and a veritable jungle to the left, teeming with songbirds chirping cheerfully, monkeys swinging energetically, fawns, frogs, tigers, rabbits… A mixture of creatures, coexisting harmoniously in the safety of the Forest. Uninhabited by humans as they knew them, the nature thrived on their land.

A faint squeaking sound diffused from a bundle of leaves that appeared to be rustling beneath a hedge, dotted with pink, purple and red flowers. Althea knelt to the floor and gently lifted the leaf that concealed a litter of new-born rabbits. She beamed at Azriel, heart warmed by their sweetness. Their eyes met, and Azriel's heart fluttered beneath his chest. Behind Althea, a rose bush was growing elegantly, and he plucked a blush-pink flower from the plant, placing it delicately in her glossy black hair.

The sun began to sink in the sky, skimming the edge of the horizon, projecting a soft, orange glow across the land and sea, and they returned to the cavern. The breeze grew ever cooler as night drew in. They passed through the hanging vines, and Azriel had been so befuddled by the waterfall earlier, he hardly noticed the oaken table and chairs, fireplace, and bamboo 4 poster bed frame, draped in silken linens that swayed in the breeze.

'Shall we catch a few fish to eat?' asked Althea.

'Yes, let's.' he agreed, suddenly feeling hungry now the adrenaline was beginning to dissolve. They strolled down to the sea front, and perched on the sand, the waves lapping at their bare feet.

'How are we going to catch fish without a fishing rod?' Azriel wondered, recalling that they were on a planet lacking in human inventions.

Althea ignored him, got up and waded knee-deep into the water. Confused, Azriel watched as she closed her eyes and rested her palms on the surface of the water. After a few short minutes, two sizable salmon fish appeared beneath her hands. She delicately traced their movements, before closing her fingers around their tails and lifting them effortlessly out of the water.

'You did not just catch two fish with your bare hands, Althea?' Azriel asked, rubbing his eyes in disbelief.

'Of all the things that have happened today, that's the part that shocks you the most?' Althea giggled, flinging the fish to him and turning back to the sea to pluck seaweed from the shallow bed.

'Well...'

'That's one thing we Omniscients have that many others lack; *patience.*' She smiled at him kindly and made for the cavern where she prepared their meal.

As they ate, they spoke of life before Calathea, as they called their new home. They spoke of the many species they have observed inhabiting Earth, the loneliness they felt, drifting aimlessly in the darkness that is outer space. Present, but not really there.

They spoke of their purpose in their new world, what they'd like to achieve-preservation of nature, harmony betwixt all creatures. They spoke deep into the night, and eventually fell to sleep on the sand, beneath the stars, side to side and barely 10 metres from the edge of the gentle ocean. The grey horse danced in the moonlight above the clouds.

Azriel woke to the sight of Althea bathing in the sea, lightly drizzling her sparkling, olive skin with clear water making her body gleam invitingly under the morning sun, dripping from her cleavage, toned midriff and defined legs.

'Good morning, Althea.' Azriel called from the shore, attempting to distract himself from the temptation spiralling from her beguiling beauty.

She turned to him with a smile.

'Sleep well?'

'Very. And you?' He replied, shielding his eyes from the rising sun.

'I did.' She said softly. 'Coming in?'

'I will.' Azriel stretched his arms above his head, and rose to his feet to wade into the water towards Althea. 'Shall we visit the Forest today?'

'Yes.' She agreed. 'Let's go deeper this time, see what else is in there.'

The pair stood, gazing out to sea for a while, before retreating to the jungle clearing. They trod carefully as they passed through the entrance to the shadowy abyss, shaped by trees creating an arch at the end of two flower-filled hedges running parallel, three metres apart to form a path.

Inside, was a picture of natural beauty. Pink blossom trees, butterflies, more white horses and so much more. Behind them, they heard hoofbeats, and turned to see Potenza, the very first creature Azriel encountered on this planet, his coat shining under a beam of the sun that was spilling through the canopy of the jungle.

The other horses formed an arc before Potenza, bent their left legs and bowed their heads to the floor. When they rose, Potenza let out a shrill whinny, and bowed back to his herd. He led them through a gap in the hedge straight ahead of them, and disappeared from sight. Azriel and Althea followed them curiously into a glorious sanctuary, home to an enormous cascade of crystal-clear water spilling from the sharp wall of rock, into the deep, blue plunge pool beneath. Encasing it, a circular border of dazzling diamonds, surrounded by dozens of pure white horses and steel grey foals, clinging to their mothers.

Awe inspired, they stood in silence, observing the scene of serenity.

Like a lead weight, a scene of sheer tragedy grounded their soaring spirits, as a foal lost his footing on the slippery rock surrounding the glowing plunge pool, he crashed to the floor. A river of blood flooded from the gaping wound caused by the jagged diamond rock he landed on. His mother snorted and pranced frantically at his side, unable to ease the plight of her baby.

Without a thought, Althea rushed to the scene, fell to her knees, and placed her hands on the infant creature's body. A soft glow of golden light radiated from her palms, engulfing the foal, drawing the blood from the ground back into the now shrinking wound. In a matter of seconds, the wound had been healed by the delicate touch of Althea's hands. A sigh of relief emanated from the brood mare, as the foal staggered to his feet, touching his pink nose to Althea's cheek, as if to thank her.

'How did you do that?' Azriel gasped, astonished by her capability.

'I.. I don't know.' She said, looking just as confused as him. 'I'd done it before I'd even thought about it. Humans don't have healing powers...'

'No, they don't. Not beyond medical science, at least.'

'If we've permanently taken human form, shouldn't we be equal to humans in our capabilities?' She asks.

'Yes, you'd think so, wouldn't you? It's perplexing. I'm beginning to think that our presence here is not as simple as it appears.' Azriel edged closer to the water, and observed the turquoise inflections in his eyes. His vision blurred for a split second, and cleared to reveal something familiar, something that he'd seen before, but not here. In a flash, the vision was gone, and he was left staring at his reflection.

Chapter 2 – Exploring New Territory

Some weeks had passed since the incident with the foal at Diamond Crescent. Uneventful, yet full of discovery. Together, Althea and Azriel explored the wonders of their modest planet, venturing deep into the forest to discover the orchards and pastures concealed by the dense clutter of trees. A sleepy village populated by friendly men, women and children lay here, with beautiful stone cottages with honeysuckle climbing the walls from flower beds beneath.

The laughter of the children echoed in the atmosphere, as they frolicked while their parents dug up potatoes. Cows, pigs and sheep dotted neighbouring fields, creating an environment fit to sustain life.

Beyond the forest they reached the scorching desert, radiating a calm ambience, contrary to the heady bustle of the forest and the creatures within. Camels ambling, kangaroos leaping, elephants sauntering. A picture of bliss.

Each ecosystem coexisted in harmony, as they once did on Earth. Different in their functions, alike in their importance. Each was as plain and simple as Earth once was, before industrial methods became customary, before mankind exploded into existence and de-naturalised nature.

While discovering the innocence and simplicity of their new home, they took time to come to a better understanding of one another. Althea revealed herself to be a mischievous and impetuous soul, yet kind and thoughtful, in constant pursuit of adventure. Her impulsiveness contradicted Azriel's rationality, his ability to consider the consequences of his actions far outshone Althea's, yet their differing attributes complemented one another. Each had something the other lacked, yet they lacked everything, without one another.

They just didn't know it yet.

Althea tried to encourage spontaneity in Azriel, derailing him from his mission to journey their entire planet in pursuit of a hint that could explain why they were there. He could not comprehend that they had been given an entire planet of their own, simply to exist peacefully. Despite her similar suspicions, Althea suggested they enjoy the present simplicity of their existence, convincing Azriel that if their purpose there was more than it seemed, it would soon reveal itself. Begrudgingly, he agreed, and they quit their expedition.

They eventually returned to their cavern, to find Potenza, master of the herd, and Pandora, mistress of the herd, swimming in the summer sea. Althea and Azriel approached the shoreline, and the horses edged toward them.

'Shall we go for a ride?' Suggested Azriel, surprising Althea with this out of character display of spontaneity.

'Have you ridden a horse before?'

'Yes. It was Potenza who first brought me to you.' Recalled Azriel.

'I can't believe the first thing you did when you got here was get on a horse. Are you sure you didn't run a risk assessment before mounting him?' She joked, a glint in her eye.

'Very funny, shall we?' He asked, gesturing toward Potenza, as if asking for permission.

'Yes, but wait a second.' Althea dashed back to their cavern, and pulled two thick vines from the entrance, which immediately replaced themselves with new ones, a slightly brighter shade of green than the others.

Althea delicately approached the horses, who offered a nod of approval when she gently placed a vine over each of their noses, crossing them at the back and looping above their ears to form a bridle, each with a large loop resting on their necks for them to use as reins. As Althea gently placed the vines down on each horse's neck, the vine bridles transformed into leather in a puff of glittery mist.

'Is there no end to your talent, Althea?' Azriel asked, continually impressed by his companion.

'It would appear not.' She smiled cheekily over her shoulder at him.

Before Azriel had time to answer, Althea had climbed to Pandora's back, perching with her right leg crossed over her neck as if riding side saddle, and they dashed into the distance at a gallop. Potenza was becoming impatient, snorting and prancing on the spot, and Azriel quickly followed suit, leaping on to his back, and gripping tightly to the reins, remembering the speed that the beast had reached the first time he rode him.

It wasn't long before they caught up with Pandora, a smaller beast than Potenza. They traced the edge of the sea for a time, before Pandora darted sharply to the left, toward to the sea, followed shortly by Potenza. Their riders braced themselves for the impact of the water, expecting to enter the sea, when instead, the staircase of clouds formed beneath their hooves, and they climbed high into the sky, gazing down at the land below them.

All too soon, the horses had tired of galloping, so they returned to ground and wandered at a steady pace into the sea, Althea and Azriel's toes skimming the surface of the water as they went. They eventually dismounted the horses and patted their solid necks, flecked with sweat.

There was a certain warmth lingering in the air, and Althea and Azriel decided to swim out to sea to cool off. Unable to stand in the depths of the ocean, Althea clung to Azriel, secretly impressed by his physicality as her hands brushed his arms and chest.

'You're going to drown me in a minute!' Gasped Azriel, 'I can't stand here either and you're heavy!' He teased, releasing her grip from his shoulders and pushing her away from him.

Althea turned to face him, and placed the palms of her hands on the surface of the water. Her gaze fixed on Azriel's shimmering blue eyes, and the water around them began to stir. In several blue ripples, it separated to reveal the white sand and dark grey rocks beneath. The pair floated down to the sea floor with the decreasing water level, and landed softly on the warm sand, surrounded by a circular wall of water, which revealed the aquarium of creatures swimming placidly along the seabed, littered with jagged rocks and seaweed, swaying sluggishly.

'You'd think with muscles like those you'd be able to carry a petite young lady like myself!' Althea remarked, breaking their piercing eye contact by wandering around the sandy breach in the ocean she'd created with her bare hands. 'Perhaps they're just for show.'

'You've noticed my muscles?' Azriel prodded, daring to hope that his sentiments may be in the slightest way returned.

Althea approached him and squeezed his right bicep with her soft hands, an ambiguous expression sweeping over her face.

'Don't flatter yourself, Azriel.'

She released her grip and lowered her hand, brushing his forearm gently with her fingertips. As her hand reached his, Azriel closed his fingers and edged closer to the woman stood opposite him. Realising that they were on the cusp of romance, Althea clicked her fingers, and the water flooded the seabed until it reached the surface, and the pair were thrust into the deep water once more.

Shocked, Azriel chased her back to the shore. They reached knee-depth, and Althea attempted to flee the ocean and seek refuge in their cavern, but Azriel was quicker than her, and reached for her arm, pulling her back towards him. They rough and tumbled in the shallow water, giggling and frolicking in each another's arms, until their eyes met.

Hallowed by sea and sand, they succumbed to the tremendous tension that had been mounting since the day they met.

The weight of their unexplored desires exploded into sexual fusion, and they plunged their lips together with a passionate kiss. Azriel caressed Althea's body, exploring the hitherto forbidden territory, his fingers melting into her skin. He gripped her thighs and wrapped her legs around his waist. Althea ran her fingers through Azriel's thick curls, and closed her hand around a lock of his hair.

Her body trembled with anticipation.

She leant back as Azriel began softly kissing her neck, tickling her skin. He advanced to her pert breasts, sea water dripping from them, and his heart slammed against his chest as the mounting anticipation began to possess him. He pushed his erect member to her groin, quickening her breath as she tasted a mere atom of the sheer pleasure he was about to inflict upon her.

Unable to withstand the anticipation any longer, he carried her to the shore and assertively pushed her body into the sand, before ripping off the silken robe that clung to her skin to unleash the beauty that it masked; revealing the indentations in her waist, the large, round breasts that now lay freely across her chest. Draped over her, he observed her beguiling nakedness for a few seconds, before tossing his own attire to the ground to expose his sizable package, rendered solid by his attraction to the gloriously naked Althea lying invitingly before him, under the sunset.

He traced her skin with his hands. Squeezing her breasts before gently nibbling on her nipples, the sensations rippling through her body driving her insane. He veered to her dripping thighs, and tickled her with his tongue, triggering positively seismic waves of pleasure through the helplessly aroused woman, who couldn't help but let out a cry of delight.

Dominated by sexual impulse, she forced his back into the sand and passionately kissed him, teasing the tip of his penis with her magically soft hand, before wrapping her mouth around it, and swirling her tongue around the tip. He groaned with satisfaction.

Convinced that she had teased him enough, she finally pressed her hands into his chest, and raised her body to sink down onto Azriel's erection. He gasped with delight as her tight, dripping volcano of pleasure clung to him.

She swung her hips in a rhythmic motion, pleasuring them both unspeakably. Sweat poured from their bodies that glistened under the last light of the sun. Gasping, Azriel plunged Althea's body to the ground, and began to thrust powerfully. Althea body began to shiver as she neared climax, inspiring Azriel to intensify her pleasure, placing her legs on his shoulders. Her muscles tensed, her body trembled, and they simultaneously climax for the first time.

They lay breathless on the sand, reflecting on their sensual awakening, and how effortless it seemed, to please each other. Their minds subconsciously knew how to perform the act that their bodies had never experienced.

As the orange glow of the sun disappeared, and the atmosphere was engulfed by darkness, Azriel stood and offered his hand to Althea, helping her to her feet. They held hands and stared adoringly into each other's eyes.

Althea inhaled to utter the words:

'I have noticed your muscles.'

They erupted into fits of laughter, and Azriel pulled her into a loving embrace, kissing her head. The evening tide began to draw in, and the cold water lapped at their toes as they lay gazing at the stars.

The next morning, they rode out to the forest, and strolled into the very heart of the orchard. Althea filled her basket with apples, oranges and pears, and filled a pale of milk from one of the brood cows, while her calf pranced about the meadow excitedly. Azriel collected timber and bamboo, intending to add to the modest infrastructure that populated their beach side home.

As she panned across the fields, observing the wildlife and the trees that rocked gently in the wind, Althea's eyes fixated on Azriel, browning in the sunlight, lifting heavy wood causing his muscles to tense most attractively. He turned to notice her watching, and joined her where she stood, on a wooden bridge connecting the land each side of the cascading river. Low hanging willow trees and colourful flowers surrounded them as the cheerful chirp of the birds sang in their ears. Ariel kissed Althea and they engaged in a romantic interlude, slowly beneath the trees.

The next few months were a whirlwind of sexual interaction, and Azriel eventually suggested they ride to Diamond Crescent, where he made a sweet revelation to her.

He took her left hand in his, and they placed them on the surface of the water.

'For so long, we have existed to benefit others, and that's all. Just existed. Now I'm here, with you, I feel that I am living. Althea, Omniscient of Compromise, your soul has been directed by another for the entirety of its existence, and I ask you now to share that soul with me for the rest of your existence?' He invited, with a genuine earnest.

'Azriel, Omniscient of Empathy, our union symbolises the freedom we now possess, to call our souls each other's.'

As they spoke, the water began to ripple, and two ribbons of water rose from the surface, spiralling a metre or so in the air. They crossed in the centre of the plunge pool and surged into the diamond encrusted edge, each breaking off a small, sparkling fragment. The ribbons of water entangled themselves and climbed so high as to reach the leaves growing from the trees towering above, raining down on Azriel and Althea.

As the droplets fell, they evolved into white petals that swarmed around the couple and landed on their skin, clothing Azriel with a fitted waistcoat with black breeches and a white neck cloth, and Althea with a laced gown, her curves accentuated by a stylish corset. The diamonds suspended in the sky shattered and pinned Althea's glossy hair into a half-up style. A band of water formed around their ring fingers, which solidified into sterling silver, and the watery ribbons encrusted a round diamond into the centre of Althea's, and a half-moon ring into Azriel's.

Pandora and Potenza emerged at the clearing of Diamond Crescent and bowed their heads to the newlyweds. They mounted the dazzling white horses, and they galloped toward the edge of the sea. They climbed the cloudy staircase higher into the sky than they had ever been, and as they levelled out and continued to travel across the fluffy surface of the sky, a large white structure became visible in the distance.

As they drew nearer, they realised it was a castle, and a magnificent one at that; a tall, white marble building with circular pillars, a triangular roof and a steep staircase leading to a large, white-washed door. It appeared to be floating inches above the white, fluffy clouds that stretched for miles in all directions. The horses slowed with the decreasing distance between them revealing the enormity of building. Pandora and Potenza came to a gentle halt.

Althea and Azriel stared at one another, utterly stunned.

Chapter 3 – The Discoveries of the Sky

'Well, this place is just full of surprises.' Remarked Althea.

'Yes.' Azriel replied. 'Well, shall we have a look around?'

Althea nodded without saying a word.

They cautiously approached the vast staircase that towered above them and climbed to the top. Azriel reached to turn the sterling silver doorknob, and the doors opened silently to expose the grand, stone interior. The hallway swept backward toward a spiralling staircase, and to the right, a dining area with a long, granite table encrusted with silver glitter. To the left, a drawing room with black faux leather seating, a large fireplace where a small pile of logs appeared to be burning out, glowing a gentle shade of orange. Candles dotted along the mantlepiece were flickering lazily as evening drew in, and the natural light spilling through the windows slowly faded.

The couple crept around the unfamiliar building.

Althea ran her fingers along the transparent white curtains that were pinned open with silken ties. She inspected the curtain rails and noticed faint scratches in the silver where the curtain rings had obviously run across the poles with the opening and closing of the curtains.

'It looks like someone has been up here.' said Althea, suddenly suspicious. 'I didn't think anybody else *could* get up here.'

What sounded like footsteps came from upstairs, and Althea and Azriel nervously approached the foot of the spiral staircase.

A silhouette appeared in the darkness. A sharp intake of breath was faintly audible from where they stood, and a glass smashed to the ground, shattering into thousands of pieces that glinted with the flicker of the candles. The silhouette drew nearer as it travelled down the stairs into the candlelight, revealing the face of Sebastian, Omniscient of Abundance.

He breathed a sigh of relief when he saw Althea and Azriel.

'You gave me such a fright!' He exclaimed, shaking Azriel's hand and kissing Althea's. 'Where did you come from?'

'The same place as you!' Giggled Althea. 'Have you been up here all this time?'

'Well, since this place exploded into existence, if that's what you mean?' Sebastian replied.

'Is it just you?' She asked again.

'Yes.' He said, suddenly looking sombre. 'Have you seen Concordia? She isn't here and I would be surprised if she was left behind.'

Althea and Azriel looked at one another.

'We haven't seen her, Sebastian.' Azriel informed him. 'We've travelled almost everywhere. She's not here.'

They were silent.

Sebastian stared solemnly for a moment, attempting to supress the terrible feeling growing in his gut and whirring in his mind.

'Where have you two been hiding all this time? What are you so dressed up for?' He asked as he refocused his gaze and suddenly noticed the tremendously glamorous outfits they were sporting.

The couple smiled sweetly at one another.

'We got married!' Althea exclaimed. 'Come with us, we'll show you what you've been missing all this time!'

She took Sebastian by the hand and led him to the door, opened it, and held it open for him and her husband. Potenza and Pandora were patiently waiting at the bottom of the staircase.

Althea and Azriel mounted Potenza, while Sebastian reluctantly took Pandora, having never ridden horseback. They steadily walked along the surface of the clouds under the sinking, evening sun. The break in the mist that revealed the staircase came into view, and Sebastian was simply amazed by the snippet of landscape that was visible through the gap.

'This has been here all this time and I had no idea what was waiting on the other side!' He beamed with sheer delight.

'You won't be disappointed.' Azriel promised.

The wind rippled through Sebastian's dark hair as they descended from the sky over the sea, and he gasped with excitement as he frantically stared about the scenery that lay before him. They touched down on the sand and came to a gradual halt. As they did, the waterfall in Azriel and Althea's cavern rained a golden shower for a few moments.

'What ever did we do to deserve this palace, I wonder?' Sebastian asked, half joking.

'Well, that is the question, actually.' Althea responded, seriously. 'We don't know why we are here. It could just be that we have been entrusted with this land simply to live, as opposed to just existing for the benefit of others. That seems too straightforward in my opinion.'

'Especially now we know you are here, and Concordia is not.' Azriel added.

'She was the last Omniscient to be called to Earth, but I don't recall her ever coming back.' Sebastian said, wrinkling his brow in thought.

'Perhaps she's still there?' Althea suggested.

'It's been a very long time.' Sebastian disagreed, the dreadful feeling in his gut came flooding back. 'None of us ever stayed that long. Admittedly, the duration we were required to stay did elongate with each visit-'

'-but never to this extent.' Azriel interrupted. 'The creatures grew vastly less cooperative as they evolved, and our task became much harder with the emergence of mankind.'

'But never did it take so long.' Althea too became concerned.

Sebastian withdrew and began to walk across the beach.

What if she never made it back?

What if something had happened to her while she was there?

He vaguely recalled the two wars that Concordia had been selected to intervene with, but he was sure that she had prevailed in restoring peace.

Perplexed, he continued to walk beneath the darkening sky, attempting to reassure himself that his fellow Omniscient was safe and well.

Somewhere.

'Azriel, I must tell you…' Althea began.

He turned to his wife, looking concerned.

'Don't look so worried!' She smiled, and directed her gaze downward. She cupped her hands held them barely a millimetre from her abdomen. A small flower grew from the palm of her hand, and her brown eyes fixated on her husband's own blue ones.

'My love, do you mean-'

She nodded with tear-filled eyes, and Azriel pulled her into a tight embrace.

They were soon to welcome a child.

He was born at dusk one chilly December evening. His emerald, green eyes captured the hearts of his adoring parents the moment they began to gleam in the evening light, an air of mischief radiating from them. It was clear to Azriel that their son would grow to embody his mother's spontaneous habits, but observed a wisdom, exceptional for one so young.

After all, he was not just any infant, but the first and only Omniscient descendant. He speculated that it would only be a matter of time before they discovered his unique ability.

'Welcome, Alexander.' Althea whispered breathlessly, as she held her child for the first time, and the waterfall in the cavern flashed gold with the arrival of this pure, sweet soul. Azriel embraced his wife and child, as the fire glowing cheerfully in the background projected a warm glow over the heavenly scene, as the sun disappeared below the horizon and darkness fell.

Next morning, Althea and Azriel introduced their son to Sebastian, who had built a cosy log cabin a few hundred yards from their cavern to live in.

'What a cherub.' He beamed, holding the young Omniscient in his arms. Turning away from his parents, Sebastian whispered to the infant, 'You, are the first Omniscient child ever to exist, young man. You'll grow up to do something extraordinary, I'm sure.' He placed a shining silver necklace over the child's head, and pressed his finger to the leaf-shaped, emerald pendant that hung from the delicate chain. The imprint resembled a Calathea, and would connect Alexander with his Omniscient family through any distance.

'I hope you won't be a bad influence on him, Sebastian.' Azriel called over his shoulder.

'Of course not!' He smirked. 'I'll teach him nothing but honesty and wisdom.'

When he was 12 weeks old, the three Omniscients journeyed to Diamond Crescent, where they held a simple ceremony to welcome Alexander. The horses and villagers gathered around the plunge pool, and the birds, squirrels and butterflies perched on the flowers and trees to view the celebration.

Althea dipped her finger in the water, which rippled and separated to form a path, and stood in the dry centre. Azriel joined her, and they placed the infant on the surface of the water, which rose into waves either side of him, lifting him into the air for the creatures to see. The random chirping of the birds harmonised into a beautiful song, and a single drop of water fell to his forehead and dripped off the end of his nose, tickling his face and making him giggle. The watery arms placed the child back into his mother's embrace, before settling back to its normal level.

Blossom petals fell from the nearby trees and floated delicately on the water as Alexander splashed his plump arms and legs around in the warm pool, while the adoring onlookers cooed at his cuteness.

Following the ceremony, the villagers joined the Omniscients at the beach, where they drank from coconuts and pineapples, and played music from bongos, castanets, and xylophones. The children ran on the sand and splashed in the sea, while Alexander watched, gleefully patting the sand and examining the shells, fascinated by the colour and texture.

'He's such a cheerful baby, Althea.' Said Rosemary Pritchard, one of the village mothers. 'Those eyes are just stunning!' She knelt to stroke his rosy cheek.

'Don't get any ideas, Rose!' Her husband, Charles Pritchard, called from across the beach. 'Two are more than enough!'

'Yes, dear!' She rolled her eyes playfully and turned, with a smile, to look at her children playing by the edge of the sea.

The celebrations continued into the night, until darkness eventually consumed the beach, and it was time to retire.

The next day, Azriel and Sebastian went to fetch some timber from the forest to build some fishing boats. First, they climbed the trees and extracted the wildlife, carrying them to safety in the neighbouring trees before cutting the chosen ones down. Once this was done, Sebastian, Omniscient of Abundance, scooped the sawdust from the ground, and sprinkled it over the tree stumps that remained. The dust hit the stumps and were thrust immediately back into the air as the trees were resurrected, the unspoilt soil capable of maintaining its own ecosystem, with a little help from the Omniscients.

'Impressive!' Azriel remarked, patting Sebastian's shoulder.

'Well, we get what we give in our world, my friend.' He replied, with a smile.

They enlisted the help of their companions from the nearby village to carry the heavy timber back to the beach. Once there, they dragged the wood across the sand and into the workshop that they had built several months earlier, along the hedgerow that lined the edge of the beach. Tools in hand, they got to work building their boats.

'Yesterday was a wonderful day.' Said Sebastian. 'I just wish Concordia were here to share it with us.'

'So do I, Sebastian.' Azriel replied thoughtfully. 'She'd have loved it. She'd love it here.'

They continued working in silence, both pondering the fate of their comrade, until their boats were finally finished. Night began to fall, and the men decided to take them for a test row before it got too dark.

They drifted along the sleepy ocean a little less than fifty metres from the shore. Azriel stared at the orange ball that was glowing what looked like inches from the surface of the sea, when his vision began to blur, until it went completely black.

He frantically felt around his small fishing boat for something to grip, as images of Concordia on Earth during World War 2 flashed before his eyes. She was thin and wounded. After a few harrowing minutes, the disturbing vision dissipated, and Azriel was left staring at the sun again, his heart hammering against his ribs.

'Azriel, is everything ok?' Sebastian asked, noticing his friend's distress.

'Fine.' He lied. 'I think I'm getting a bit drowsy, better get back to shore.'

Sebastian struggled to keep up with Azriel as he raced back to the shore and hurried back to his cavern, closing the door behind him without a word.

He stood behind the closed door, staring blankly and breathing heavily.

Althea was sat at the table with their son on her lap, dancing him on her knee.

'Who's that, Alexander?' She asked in a high-pitched voice as the baby giggled. 'Is it daddy?' She smiled up at her husband, noticing his strange behaviour.

'Azriel, what is it?'

'I'm not sure.' He began. 'I was just staring out to sea and then I saw it…'

'It?'

'I saw Concordia. She was hurt.' Azriel continued.

'She's here? Where is she, Azriel? Did Sebastian take her home with him?' Althea asked, half panicking and half relieved by the prospect that Concordia was there with them in Calathea.

'No, no she's not here.' Azriel sat at the table. 'As you know, I have the ability to alter perspective, to encourage empathy towards others, using my eyes. Well, that's how it worked when I went to Earth.'

'But?' Althea encouraged her husband to continue, perching on the edge of the seat adjacent to his, on the short edge of the rectangular table.

'Since we've been here, I've been having visions. I've been seeing things that I've seen before on Earth. Today I saw Concordia. I'm not sure if she's there now or if my vision was from the past.'

'You say she was hurt?' Althea asked, growing increasingly concerned.

'Yes, she didn't look well at all. I can't understand why she wasn't recalled to space, or why none of us were sent to help her!' Azriel stood up and began to pace around the cavern. Alexander cried as his father walked past him, ignoring his flailing arms requesting to be picked up.

'Should we tell Sebastian?'

'Absolutely not.' Azriel said sternly, picking Alexander up to stop him from crying. 'He's already very worried about her I don't want to alarm him even more. Not until we know exactly what has happened to her.'

Chapter 4 – Alexander's Uprising

Alexander grew to embody the best of his parents' attributes. He was thoughtful and wise as his father, yet adventurous and spontaneous like his mother. The glow of his green eyes only got brighter with every year of his life, and he grew very close to Sebastian.

'We didn't always live here, you know, kid.' Sebastian told the 10-year-old boy, as they rowed from the shore to do some fishing. 'There was a time when your parents and I had a great responsibility to a place called Earth.'

'What did you do there?' Alexander asked eagerly, his green eyes shining with anticipation.

'Well, if the creatures there got into big fights and couldn't get along, we would go and help them sort it all out so they could live happily again.' Sebastian simplified. 'One day you'll do something just as, if not *more* important, young Alexander-you mark my words! But for now, let's catch some dinner!' He flicked the child with water as he rowed further out to sea.

'Hey! You got me!' he squealed playfully, picking up his own ores and rowing after him.

They returned to shore a few hours later, Alexander soaked with sea water and grinning from ear to ear.

'Mama, look what I caught!' He beamed, running toward Althea holding a fish that must've been a foot long.

'Wow, look at that! Have you been swimming?' She asked, stroking his dripping hair.

'Uncle Sebastian pushed me in!' He screeched, pointing at the sheepish Omniscient.

'Sebastian, how many times-'

'Oh, he loves it, Althea. He can swim, can't he?' He grinned, ruffling the boy's hair, splashing all 3 of them with water. He pinched the fish from his hand and ran off. 'This looks nice, I think I'll have this one instead!'

'No, Uncle Sebastian! Come back!' The boy chased after him, and Azriel emerged from their cavern to stand arm in arm with his wife.

'What are we going to do with those two, Althea?' He smiled.

'Heaven only knows, Azriel.' She laid her head on his shoulder as Alexander and Sebastian gambled about the sand under the pink sky.

In his early teens, Alexander taught the village children to fish and to ride. He visited the forest and orchards often, where he found a puppy that had strayed from his mother, who was nowhere to be found, and so decided to take him back to the cavern.

'Who's this?' Althea asked, noticing the excitable, fluffy ball in his hands as he entered.

'This is…' He held the animal up to get a better look at his stone-coloured face, with a wide forehead, floppy ears and the kindest eyes, enhanced by small patches of white fur above them. 'Wilbur.'

Althea held out her hand so as to introduce herself to the puppy, who sniffed and nibbled gently on her fingers.

'He's very sweet.' She giggled. 'Where did you find him?'

'He was curled up under an apple tree, all alone.' He snuggled the creature to his cheek. 'I looked for his mother, but she was nowhere to be seen. I couldn't just leave him there.'

'Of course not.' She agreed passionately. 'He's your responsibility, sweetheart. Remember that.'

He did indeed remember that. Wilbur and Alexander did everything together. He built a platform at the bow of his boat for Wilbur to sit on while he reeled in fish for supper, and he ran alongside Alexander and his horse as they cantered along the shore.

Wilbur was Alexander's shadow. One did not exist without the other since the day he found him curled up at the trunk of an apple tree.

There was no denying the purity and kindness of Alexander's soul, but what about his unique Omniscient talent?

'He's 17 now, Althea. I was sure he'd have established his Omniscience by now.' Azriel said, a concerned twinge to his tone, as he and his wife strolled on horseback through the forest.

'Well, what further abilities does he need?' Althea asked, shaking her head and shrugging. 'He's kind and considerate, he cares for all the creatures he encounters, great and small. Most of all, he's *happy*, Azriel.'

'Yes, but-'

'My love,' She leant across Pandora's back and took Azriel's hand. 'Being an Omniscient means something different now. We're not puppets anymore. Our duty isn't to Earth any longer, it is to Calathea. To ensure our people do not make the same mistakes as they did on Earth, to allow greed and brutality to be the marks of a gentleman or gentlewoman. We are here to demonstrate that all creatures can live in harmony, allow each another access to exactly what we all require, and have a care for one another. Alexander is capable of that, and I think this is now what it means to be Omniscient.'

'Surely he has some kind of ability that sets him apart from humanity.' Azriel challenged.

'Absolutely he does.' Althea chuckled. 'The ability to listen, to be patient, to simply live in the moment and be grateful for all that is beautiful and to accept others for all that they are, no more and no less. You do him a disservice, Azriel.'

Azriel sighed, a faint concern in his eyes. They continued to ride in silence as he realised there was no convincing Althea that her son had not yet displayed a special ability, as each Omniscient before him had done.

What they had not noticed, was Alexander and Wilbur picking apples nearby, just close enough to grasp the general concept of the conversation between his parents. He slumped against a tree and slid to the ground, feeling hurt that he had disappointed his father, when all he had ever done was try to please him. Wilbur jumped into his lap and planted several slobbery licks onto his cheek, and barked shrilly, noticing how downcast his companion had suddenly become.

He forced a weak giggle and held the fervent puppy in the air, just above his head.

'What would I do without you, Wilbur?' The dog barked as if to answer him, and Alexander decided to find Sebastian. He began to walk, and Wilbur ran in circles around his heels, enthused by the prospect of an adventure.

He found Sebastian sat by the edge of the sea, the waves just reaching his toes as the water rose and fell. Wilbur spotted him and raced towards him, trampling his lap, flinging sand and sea water into his face.

'Thank you, Wilbur.' He said through pursed lips, wiping the salt water out of his eyes. 'Where's Alexander, then?'

A few moments later, Alexander threw himself onto the sand a few feet from his dear friend, Sebastian.

'What's the matter, young man?' He asked, noticing the miserable look on Alexander's face.

He sighed heavily.

'I overheard a conversation I suspect my mother and father would have preferred me not to hear.'

'Oh?' Sebastian enquired, as Wilbur nibbled at his toes and chased the water.

'Father is disappointed in me. He thinks I'm... ordinary. More like a human than an Omniscient.' Alexander replied, avoiding eye contact with Sebastian, as if he were ashamed of the words spilling from his mouth.

Sebastian turned to him, met with the side of his face. He was devastated to think that such a remarkable young man could be made to feel inferior, particularly by his own parent.

'You listen to me, Alexander. Look at me.' Sebastian directed, a determined strength in his voice. 'Your mother, father and I have seen all there is to see about humans. We observed them for centuries. I've never been overly impressed, but you... I've known you a mere 17 years in comparison, and I am continually impressed by the very essence of your being. You are far from ordinary. Light years ahead of humanity.'

Alexander smiled at him through watery eyes. Sebastian ruffled his hair and patted his arm.

'The best is yet to come, young man. I've said it before and I'll continue to say it until I am *blue in the face*, we Omniscients once had a great responsibility to Earth, but one day... One day you'll do something just as, if not more important. Don't you forget it!' He cried jubilantly, it was obvious how much he adored the teenager, and the genuine belief he had in him.

Althea watched them from the door of her cavern, catching the last of Sebastian's words of encouragement to her son, grinning proudly. Azriel approached her from behind, placing his hands on her waist and kissing her neck.

'You see? All you have to do is believe in him.' She turned to face her husband, wrapping her hands around his neck. He traced the silken night dress complementing her hourglass figure. 'Do you think you could turn your attention to another task this evening?' She kissed him gently. 'Perhaps you could… attend to your wife?'

Her eyes twinkled temptingly, and Azriel took his invitation to romance her, lifting her from the ground and wrapping her body closely around his. He placed her gently on the table, teasing her body most satisfyingly. Her gentle moans guided him to undress, and he began gently thrusting as orange flames flickered softly beside them.

Before he knew it, Alexander's 18th birthday was upon him, and he decided to host a party on the beach. He wanted to decorate the porch of the cavern with a bamboo awning and leafy bunting, so he made for the outskirts of the desert lands, enlisting the aid of his horse, Phoenix, for the journey. The wind surged through his wavy hair as they travelled at an impressive speed toward their destination.

When they arrived, Alexander examined the selection of trees growing before him, running his fingers along each of them to test for strength. He found one that wasn't too strong, but just durable enough for the purpose, and closed his hand around it, reaching for the axe he brought to chop it down with, until…

'Ouch!' He cried, as he tore the bamboo tree out of the ground with one hand, and hit himself on the head with it as he fell. The pendant hanging from his neck flickered an emerald glow.

The hole the tree left in the ground began to fill itself in with soil, and a new tree stem shot up, as if to replace the one in Alexander's hand.

He struggled to his feet and stared at the bamboo tree balancing in his hand, utterly stunned.

'How on Calathea did I do that?' He muttered to himself. 'It must've been dead already… surely.'

He dropped the tree in his hand and lunged forward to the nearest one he could find, wrapped his hand around it and tugged. Sure enough, the tree came right out of the ground, and a new stem emerged from the soil. For several minutes he stood confused, wondering how he suddenly had the ability to literally pull trees from the ground. Roots and all.

Then, he remembered all the occasions he and Sebastian had gone to collect firewood, and he simply sprinkled sawdust over the stump of the tree, and it had resurrected before their very eyes. Alexander had tried countless times to perform such a miracle, but had until now, been unsuccessful.

Spirits soaring, he tied the bamboo trees to his back, and galloped back to the beach, where his parents' cavern stood.

Unable to contain his excitement, he hopped off of Phoenix's back before he had even come to a halt, and sprinted toward the cavern. His parents stepped out of the door and he ground to a stop, sand spraying as he skidded.

'Someone's in a hurry!' Althea laughed, examining his flushed cheeks and restless demeanour. 'What're you up to, birthday boy?'

Alexander took a deep breath and was about to spill his incredible realisation to them, but before the words could fall out of his mouth, he contemplated revealing his newfound strength, his *Omniscience*, in an elaborate display later that evening.

'J-Just some decorations for later.' He stuttered, before smiling and getting to work.

The blue sky grew dark as evening crept in, and Alexander's guests began to gather on the beach, dotted with small, bamboo tables filled with tumblers of fruit punch, a campfire in the centre surrounded by logs and blankets. The area was fenced by a bamboo awning, roofed by large green leaves. Fireflies buzzed around lazily, illuminating the darkened beach and glittering over the sea, while the scene was serenaded by flutes, harmonicas and bongos.

Sebastian approached Alexander with a huge smile on his face, and shoved a fruit punch into his hand.

'Happy birthday, young man.' He put his arm around him and patted his back affectionately.

'Thanks, Uncle Sebastian.' He beamed back at him.

After an hour or so of mingling, chatter and laughter, Alexander gathered his guests around the fire.

'As a special thank you to each of you here this evening, I wanted to show you something…'

He lifted a Queen Cockleshell from the sand, lined with multicoloured vertical stripes, held it to the sky, and the glint in his eye shot out into the shell in his hand. The rectangular edge lit up, and the light travelled along each of the vertical ribbons of colour until they reached the top of the shell and burst forth into the sky in the form of fireworks whistling, crackling and popping in the air with dazzling colour and light.

Azriel beamed with pride as he watched his son's Omniscient talents unfold before his very eyes. Uncontrollable clapping filled the beach as the people that had watched him grow into the special young man that stood before them this evening, witnessed him find his powers.

The property of each Omniscient's ability stems from their perspective, their values, and their character, and comes in many forms. Alexander strives to see the brightness in times of dark, goodness in what is bad, and embodies an impressive strength of character. The ability to separate himself from negativity. His abilities would reflect such qualities and were yet to be truly uncovered.

'How's that for ordinary, father?' Alexander joked, raising his eyebrow.

The colour drained from Azriel's face.

'Alexander-'

'You don't have to say anything.' He interjected. 'At least somebody had faith in me.' He turned his gaze to Sebastian, and patted his father on the shoulder, before walking away.

Azriel's heart sank, dismayed to think that he left a void in Alexander's heart that Sebastian had stepped in to fill.

Althea noticed what happened and approached her husband with a kiss on the cheek, hugging his waist.

'He's right, you know. I tried to tell you.' She said. 'All you had to do was believe in him.'

'I realise that now.' Azriel admitted. 'And thanks to my ignorance, I think he now favours Sebastian. Above his own father. And it is all my fault.'

Althea cupped her hand to his cheek.

'In all your time on Earth, did you ever hear the phrase "it takes a village to raise a child"?' She said softly.

'Yes.' He replied defeatedly.

'Well, look around you!' She laughed, spinning with her arms outstretched, gesturing toward the entire village that had shown up in honour of their son, out of sheer adoration for the wonderful young man he had become. 'No parent is perfect, Azriel. Not even an Omniscient one. We, like humans, are flawed. What matters is our ability to recognise our flaws, and to learn from them.'

A smile forced its way across Azriel's lips, despite his best efforts to remain neutral.

'You, are the solution to everything, my love.' He held both of Althea's hands in his and kissed her knuckles. 'You're like our son. You always see the bright side.'

'Alexander!' Althea called, gesturing for him to join them with her hand.

'Happy birthday, my dear. Your father and I are so very proud of you.' She kissed his cheek.

Alexander placed an arm on each of his parent's shoulders. Noticing the sweet scene, Sebastian raised his glass and yelled:

'To Alexander!'

'Alexander!' The congregation repeated, and the evening continued for several hours before it drew to a contented close.

Chapter 5 - Meanwhile on Earth

2022

NASA Goddard Space Flight Center, MD, United States.

'Sir, may I speak with you?' Asked Eleanor Johnson, head of Earth Observatory for National Aeronautics and Space Administration. A tall, slender, blonde lady, with piercing blue eyes. She wore a navy-blue pencil skirt with a loose, white shirt tucked into it. Her hair was unattentively scraped into a claw clip, and her square glasses magnified the concerned look in her eyes.

'What is it, Johnson?' Snapped Chief Scientist William Hickory, frustratedly holding his hand over the microphone of his receiver.

'I'm sorry to interrupt you, I can see that you're very busy.' Ellie ignored his abrasiveness, she had something very important to unveil. 'But there's not a moment to lose, our Junior Observer has made a discovery which requires our immediate attention.'

Hickory considered for a moment… 'Mr Barnes, I'll have to call you back, something urgent has come up.' He slammed the telephone on to the rack and stood to face Ellie. 'This better be important…Eleanor.' He warned, peering at her name badge to remind himself of her forename. Johnson nodded, and strode purposefully toward the Earth Observatory quarter, Hickory in tow.

'Mr Samson and his team have been tracking the Earth's path over the past decade, Jonny, go ahead.'

'Mr Hickory,' Jonny nodded respectfully, and shook William's hand. 'Thank you for your time. As we know, the Earth has migrated approximately 1.5cm away from the sun each year for the past billion years, as a result of it burning its own energy, thereby losing power, mass and gravity. This weakening in gravity causes the Earth to slowly move away from it. This pattern has dissolved gradually over the past 10 years, whereby the Earth has begun to migrate back toward the sun at an alarmingly rapid rate, and we have not yet found an explanation for this. All we know is, in 2020, Earth was positioned approximately 151.77 million kilometres from Earth. Today, 1st January 2022, we are 148.23 million kilometres from the sun. The theory that Earth would collide with the sun during it's red giant phase in 7 billion years has been disregarded, and we are currently recalculating this time frame.'

'Dear God.' Gasped Hickory, staring worriedly at the screen before him, mapping the Earth's migration toward the sun. 'What can we do?'

'At this stage, it's too early to say, as we do not yet have a clear indication of how much quicker we expect Earth to be absorbed by the sun. We have begun working on the possibility of inhabiting another planet in the Solar system, and interestingly, have observed a foreign presence in the solar system that we only identified very recently. We do not yet know exactly when this planet formed, but have so far detected indications of life on this planet that are remarkably similar to that of Earth. We will be launching an investigation into the possibility of humanity inhabiting this planet. We have already designated a team of engineers to develop a space shuttle in anticipation of travelling to the planet, once we have more information.' Explained Samson.

'I want an update as to every stage of this investigation, and I want to know as soon as you have calculated a new time frame.' Directed Mr Hickory.

Samson nodded, returning to his computer screen.

Hickory and Johnson left the room, and began talking in the corridor.

'Is that kid up to this task, Johnson?' Asked a sceptical Hickory. 'We're talking about the future of mankind, not choosing who you want to play on your football team during lunch break.'

'Mr Hickory, Samson may be young, but I've never seen a more skilled Earth Science Outreach Specialist. He knows what he's doing.' She assured him, taken aback by his cynicism.

Hickory shook his head and began to walk back to his office.

'We're not just talking about the future of mankind, Mr Hickory.' Eleanor called after him. He continued without a backward glance. 'We're talking about the future of the Earth.' She scowled at the back of his head, disappearing down the hallway, and returned to her office…

'Azriel… Azriel… are you alright?' Althea shook her husband, who lay unconscious, with his eyes open, the turquoise inflections glowing blindingly, expanding and contracting, as if zooming in and out.

'Althea, it's happening.' Azriel gasped, panic stricken. 'The humans on Earth are planning to invade Calathea. The Earth is moving rapidly toward the sun and they don't know how much longer it will be safe to live there. They want to move mankind to Calathea.'

The colour drained from Althea's face, as the reality they had feared for many years began to take shape.

'You saw it?' She asked gravely.

'I saw it. They're working out how much longer Earth will be safe for, and have recognised life on Calathea to be similar to that of humanity. I don't yet know how long we have before they are able to enter.'

'What do we do? Do we allow them?'

'I do not know.' Azriel paused for a few thoughtful moments. 'We need to keep track of what's going on over there.'

'How?' She asked, confused.

'Is everything ok?' Asked Sebastian cheerfully, unaware of the tremendous anxiety building between Althea and Azriel. 'What's wrong?' He asked again, noticing their troubled expressions.

Before they had time to answer their friend, the blue, sunny sky turned crimson.

'What's that?' Sebastian pointed to the sky, and everyone looked up to see a shiny object ripping through the sky at a sickening speed. They had visions of the glass ball smashing to the ground and shattering before their very eyes as it drew ever nearer, with no sign of slowing down. Sure enough, just metres from the floor, the object came to an abrupt halt, the impact generating a strong breeze in the air.

The Omniscients edged closer to the foreign object, staring cautiously among each other.

From space, Anad pressed his right index finger into an indent in the glass ball known as the Omni, revealing a rotary dial. He rotated his finger anti-clockwise, until the image radiating from the glass ball displayed a slideshow of evolution, displaying Earth from it's very beginning, up to present day, rolling before their very eyes in a mere few seconds. The slideshow began with the earliest Eon in Earth's history, the Pre-Omniscient period, more commonly referred to as the Precambrian period which existed over 4 billion years ago, starting with the Earth's creation.

The Omni lit up like a disco ball while the Omniscients watched. A star in space collapsed, disturbing a cluster of dust that began to spin frantically and compact in the dense vacuum, to form an enormous round solid.

The dial began to spin clockwise as a scene of destruction filled the glass ball; a protoplanet collided into Earth and asteroids bombarded the planet, instilling life-enabling stores of water into its crust. The Omni glowed red as the crust of the Earth consisted primarily of molten magma, which cooled to pave the way for volcanoes to form. Furious eruptions ejected boulders and ash and lava from the conical structures, but more importantly, the atmosphere as we know it began to form gradually, as Carbon Dioxide, Oxygen and water vapour filled the air from the volcanic eruptions.

The dial slowed as the dark and ashy atmosphere brightened with the cooling of the molten magma and decreasing frequency of volcanic eruptions. The heavy, red glow was replaced by a soft blue radiance as liquid ocean spilled into formation. As such, the Precambrian Era ended with the emergence of celled life, where the creatures from the first organisms to exist (bacteria) evolved into the first aquatic species including fish, corals and even the first land plants that the Earth ever birthed.

The Earth remained unencumbered by the presence of Omniscients until life forms became more complex during the Devonian era, which occurred in the Phanerozoic Eon. The Omni showed aquatic creatures emerging from the water and evolving into all kinds of reptiles that conquered the land and gave rise to all amphibious and land creatures.

The rotary dial stopped spinning and the Omni replayed a scene in real time; the ferocious conflict from 350 million years ago, between the amphibious creatures and the land reptiles, where the reptiles brutally attacked the amphibians attempting to deviate from the water and walk their land. The bruised and beaten carcasses of amphibians and reptiles alike, littered the ground as the first Omniscient ever to grace the planet, Azriel, Omniscient of Unity, swept through the Ozone layer, and transformed from a transparent shadow into the form of a species much larger than those already populating the land.

Azriel became green in colour, with a long, thick tail and elephant-like feet. He landed on the ground, and in sheer amazement, the creatures fighting around him paused and stared. Azriel lifted his tail and whipped it to the ground with a sickening crack that shook the Earth with such force, the living and dead creatures surrounding him were thrust into mid-air, suspended for several seconds. They were temporarily under Azriel's influence, and he guided each and every living creature to the edge of the water, where they each stared at their own reflections. Azriel bewitched the water so that their reflections changed, making each creature identical in appearance. He wished to make them see that while they were different in their capabilities and physical form, they were alike in their susceptibility to pain and entitlement to walk the land or swim the water at leisure.

After a few moments, those that survived stared about the tragic scene, corpses strewn across the edge of the water, and the reptiles allowed the amphibians to walk the land among them, as equals.

Satisfied that they could exist peacefully and continue to allow one another to cross the boundary between land and water, he was recalled to space by Anad, his obligation was discharged.

The rotary dial began to spin again as time fast forwarded through the ages, seeing all feuds that had arisen being healed by the intervention of Omniscients, but more importantly, the cooperation of the species.

Althea, Omniscient of Compromise, was called to Earth to settle a dispute between the four most prominent species to exist during the Permian period, 200 million years ago. This was a time where there were no countries, and the Earth consisted of one large land mass, surrounded by an enormous body of water. The four species, the Mesosaurus, Cynognathus, Lystrosaurus and Glossopteris, had overpopulated one small corner of the land mass named Pangaea.

Since they had all settled there since the beginning of their existence, there was a terrible dispute over which species would move out to inhabit a new territory. The issue was exacerbated by the ever-growing population of each species. Althea entered the Earth and dropped a blade that ripped through the sky at a dizzying speed as it fell. It landed in the middle of the altercation, and enormous cracks appeared in between each group of species. The land mass separated, with the oceanic water filling the expanding gaps. Some species ended up getting lost in the wrong land mass, but were accepted by the alternate species as an old friend.

Althea's blade melted into the water, and evaporated into mist, rising back to space. Their harmonious existence flashed by as the rotary dial sped up once again.

Next to appear, the battle of the food shortage between the first dinosaurs and first mammals ever to inhabit the Earth, cured by Sebastian, Omniscient of abundance, 150 million years ago. He entered the Earth and took the form of a seed, which multiplied into thousands of seeds that scattered across the ground, and instantly grew into enough plants to sustain all life on Earth.

Sebastian's own seed took the form of the first bird to exist on the planet. He opened his wings, which glowed as he shed a layer of his feathers, that floated to the ground delicately.

Before they touched down, each one transformed into a different species of bird. The first flowering plants and lush green trees shot out of the ground, decorating the edge of the large body of water the creatures drank from. The Earth's plain and simple appearance was transformed into a colourful grandeur, and Sebastian observed the evolving creatures from the skies, until he too was recalled to space, having successfully restored tranquillity to the Earth once more.

The more evolved a species became, however, the more difficult they became to reason with, and the Omni grew darker as time rolled on; the emergence of humans saw the feuds that plagued the Earth grow more violent and more deadly, fuelled by greed and hate.

The first Omniscient to be called to Earth to reason with mankind, was Althea. The Omni glowed a furious shade of red as blood-soaked victims of the Nataruk massacre, the earliest deadly conflict among humanity in 8000 BC, lay dying at the edge of Lake Turkana, Kenya.

Althea took the form of a dark-skinned woman, with deep brown, kind eyes and braided black hair. She placed her hands on the dusty dirt upon which the victims lay, and a golden glow rolled across the ground beneath them, engulfing their bodies. The Earth opened up and buried them into separate graves. Grass rolled over them and vibrant flowers stemmed from where their bodies lay, symbolic of the circle of life.

Althea spoke with the few survivors, and learned that the assailants had attacked them and stolen their food supplies, as there was a deadly shortage ravaging through civilisation. Sebastian joined Althea, and they worked to plant crops in neighbouring settlements, in the hope that this generation, and generations to come could live peacefully, with all the resources they needed to survive. Sebastian and Althea retreated.

As the rotary dial continued to wind clockwise, Anad and the Omniscients observed each generation of humanity, and realised that as they evolved, they didn't *need* anything more than they had, not just to survive, but to live…They simply *wanted* more and more as time ticked on, each of their desires becoming more costly to all. It began with arrows shot from bows, followed by swords and eventually guns, along with bombs destroying the land and poisoning the air.

The abolition of slavery pioneered by Concordia, Omniscient of Empathy, was simply not enough to eliminate this crime from the Earth, the now illegal atrocity still occurring today. This failing was merely the beginning of her tragic end…

They all watched as 1945 rolled into view, the last time Anad sent an Omniscient spirit to Earth. Concordia. The first Omniscient spirit to be eternally destroyed. She was deployed to Earth to influence the end of the Second World War, and her demise led Anad to a decision.

Unspeakable images of destruction filled the spherical glass, ancient and distinguished buildings reduced to useless piles of rubble. Worthy human beings dispatched by the most brutal means imaginable. Those that survived, in states so miserably poor. The wounds they sustained to their bodies would heal, but those sustained to their mind would plague them for as long as they lived on Earth.

The poignant images faded to reveal the Omniscient commander Anad and his spouse, Prima discussing Concordia's defeat on the day that they created Calathea all those years ago.

'Prima, it's time.' Anad spoke solemnly. 'Concordia was our last hope. Since her soul was so callously destroyed, we cannot risk sending another Omniscient to Earth to walk among humanity. We must act. Peace will never be achieved while humans exercise their self-proclaimed supremacy, violating the purity of nature and the loyalty of its creatures.'

'What is to be done?' Prima asked, nodding in accord.

'Concordia is the first Omniscient to have been unsuccessful in restoring peace to the inhabitants of the Earth.' Anad shook his head in disbelief. 'And the first to have been destroyed.'

The spirit of Concordia rose from the glass ball and exploded into a shower of golden glitter. Once the glitter had settled, the image of Anad's face filled the Omni once more, and he spoke directly to the bewildered onlookers.

'Omniscients.' He began, his voice deep as the Ocean that lay beside them, the waves gathering height as time continued. 'I applaud the equilibrium among all creatures and ecosystems that you have maintained during your time in Calathea. I imagine you are curious as to why I collided the souls of Azriel, Omniscient of Unity, Althea, Omniscient of Compromise, and Sebastian, Omniscient of Abundance, to create the land of new beginnings. As you now know, the soul of Concordia was destroyed during her efforts to cease World War 2.' As he spoke, the Omni displayed the footage of her last moments on Earth, cradled in the arms of another in a state just as poor as herself. 'Man's inhumanity to man, combined with the ever-sophisticating artillery is the biggest crisis Earth has ever seen. I'm sure you all recall the increasing difficulty you experienced when mediating with the species inhabiting the evolving Earth, but it does not compare to the spiralling defiance of mankind. As Omniscient commanders of harmonious coexistence, we have reached a decision.' Anad took Prima's hand, directing his gaze into her eyes. They nodded in agreement, and Anad continued. 'We cannot direct the extinction of humanity. This would pose a violation against nature which is precisely the opposite of what the Omniscients stand for. Instead, we opted to work with nature, by way of hastening Earth's engulfment by the sun, and starting afresh with Calathea.'

The Omni flickered, displaying Anad blowing the Earth's course toward the sun.

'The process will be complete in a matter of years,' Anad continued. 'In the meantime, you should keep inhabitants of Earth from entering Calathea by any means you see fit.'

Anad's voice faded, and the colour drained from the Omni. Before anyone could say anything, it shot into the sky, lifting the veil of darkness it brought as it climbed. The sea calmed and the comforting blue of the sky was restored as the Omni disappeared into space.

The Omniscients were silent for what seemed like an age.

'She's… dead.' Sebastian murmured. 'Concordia is dead.'

Althea embraced the broken man, tears streaming down her cheeks as the crushing suspicions that had plagued her for weeks were confirmed.

'What's going on?' Alexander asked as he emerged from the forest. 'What was that thing in the sky?'

'I must inform you all, that I have the ability to tune into Earth using my eyes. Only today I had a vision that mankind have been tracking the Earth's course toward the sun. They have recognised Calathea as a place compatible with human life and are exploring the possibility of inhabiting it before the Earth is absorbed by the sun.'

'What can we do?' Asked Alexander, a curious and adventurous soul, just like his mother.

The Omniscients all turned to Azriel for guidance.

Realising it was down to him to lead the charge against invasion, he articulated the plan he had been pondering for some time.

'Someone must go to Earth.'

Chapter 6 – An Unexpected Guest

After much deliberation, the Omniscients decided that Alexander would be crossing through the realm of peril, to divert the earthly mission to inhabit Calathea. Having never visited Earth nor contended with its inhabitants, they decided an unbiased perception and his unique, plentiful Omniscient talent would render him the most successful candidate for the task.

Althea was reluctant, at first, to surrender her only son to the mercy of planet Earth, worrying that his trusting nature and lack of experience with people would derail him. She then remembered that he was an Omniscient, a powerful one at that, and they should trust him to complete the task. Perilous though it may be.

Recalling how he had once been summoned to Earth by Anad, Azriel plucked a shimmering stone from the water at Diamond Crescent, and the Omniscients gathered around the waterfall in the cavern.

Althea hugged her son tightly. Through tear filled eyes, she took a good look at his handsome face, kissed the imprint of his necklace, and nodded to gesture that she was ready to let him go.

Alexander took the stone from his father, held it above his head, and stepped into the waterfall. The flow of the liquid quickened as it engulfed his body, and a white light shone from the stone, refracting toward the Earth as the vacuum of space opened, and Alexander disappeared in a blinding flash that soared into outer space. He reached the Ozone Layer of the Earth, and passed into the atmosphere as the light transformed into a parachute that lowered Alexander to the ground gently. He noticed he was not wearing the clothing he had dressed himself in- he was now sporting a white, long sleeved 'Ralph Lauren' shirt, the sleeves rolled neatly to just below his elbows, with smart black jeans and black leather shoes.

Maryland, USA

Alexander's heart thudded against his chest and his palms were damp. He gazed about his unfamiliar surroundings, cars and lorries speeding past him, horns sounding, children laughing, dogs barking- it was a chaos that he wasn't accustomed to, but he knew he had to keep his composure.

He drew a deep breath, blew it out, and tried to gather the thoughts racing around his mind. To his left, he noticed a sign that read 'NASA Goddard Space Flight Centre'. The whirring in his brain slowed as he began to focus on his mission, and he made for the large, white building.

He approached the door guarded by a tall, large man dressed in a navy suit with his hands behind his back.

'Show me your badge, sir.' The man directed, without even looking at Alexander.

'I... I... uh-' He began to panic.

'Your ID badge that proves you work here?' The security guard elaborated, sarcastically.

'Oh, right, no I don't work here. I just thought I could come and look around?' He asked hopefully.

The security guard chuckled and moved so he was completely blocking the closed door.

'This isn't a museum, sir. Please back away from the building.'

Alexander paused for a second before nodding and walking away.

'No need to worry.' He whispered to himself, worried.

I have just arrived, he thought, there was no way I was going to figure all this out right away. I'll get in somehow. I suppose I should work out where I'm going to live while I'm here.

Despite his attempts to calm himself, his nerves were frayed and his mood fractious. He was unable to think straight with the unfamiliar surroundings and noises jumping out at him as he stepped cautiously along the 'sidewalk' of a busy road.

He walked and walked until he encountered a footpath that led him away from industrial civilisation and toward the countryside. He followed a river trickling rather calmingly alongside the trees and felt more collected the further from the city he got.

Alexander reached a cosy nook in between two oak trees, a rural cul-de-sac. He decided he would assemble lodgings for himself in this small, secluded area for his stay on Earth.

He collected handfuls of pebbles from the bed of the river and threw them up into the air. Before they began to descend, they grew into large, square bricks, charcoal in colour. They slotted into one another to form a small lodge.

Grooves began to appear in the stone which quickly developed into a door and two small windowpanes on either side. Alexander threw a handful of sandy dust from beneath his feet into the window shaped gaps in the stone, which caught fire in mid-air and melted into windows that slotted effortlessly into the panes.

Inside, a wooden bed frame and a table and chairs populated the small space, with a small fireplace in between. He noticed a cotton handkerchief in the left pocket of his trousers and held two corners in both hands up to his mouth. He blew a breath of air beneath the small square of white fabric, releasing fibres as it flapped in the artificial breeze. As the fibres landed, a thick duvet rolled neatly across the bed, and one particularly large particle burst into a bouncy pillow.

The talented Omniscient then proceeded to brush the skin of his left forearm with the handkerchief, before folding it neatly and placing it on his bed. The handkerchief rose as a selection of clothing that folded itself beneath.

Admiring his handywork, he picked up his magical handkerchief and returned it to his pocket. Noticing the blue-sky darkening, Alexander collected firewood from some nearby trees, and settled for the evening.

When he woke the next morning, he took out a book that his father had handed him before he left Calathea. Azriel had composed a description of the vision he had from Earth, explaining what he saw, and the discoveries humanity had made in relation to the new planet. Familiarising himself with his task, he pondered how he would possibly get into the organisation with guards at the entrance. Unable to solve his quandary, he wished his father was there to guide him with his unwavering wisdom. He also thought that though Sebastian was mischievous, he had often helped him to overcome difficulties in the most unconventional ways.

'What would Sebastian do?' He sighed, racking his brain and hopelessly flicking his book shut.

A few weeks passed, and Alexander was no closer to entering NASA's location without an ID card. He felt defeated, recalling all the stories he had been told of his Omniscient family completing their Earthly missions almost immediately after they arrived on the planet. He also remembered them telling him how much more difficult their tasks became as time ticked on, particularly since humanity walked the Earth.

'What if this is too great a task for me?' He asked himself.

It was all too much. He hadn't chosen this mission; he was elected by his fellow Omniscients who deemed him the most powerful of them all. If this was true, why wasn't he making any progress?

He decided to return to NASA's headquarters to try his luck again, walking from the comfort of his chambers to the unfamiliar loudness of the inner city. He passed many homeless people, dressed in rags littered with holes and dirt, with straggly facial hair and shivering in the cold breeze. He wondered how things had gotten like this, why were people disregarded and left to freeze and starve on the side of the road, while others strolled past sporting designer attire and eating steaming, hot food?

A pang of sadness smacked his soul as he realised why Anad had made the decision to start afresh on Calathea. The closer he got to his destination, the less homeless people he encountered, and he directed his thoughts to his task. He took a deep breath as the building came into view, attempting to supress his nerves.

As he approached, he noticed a young woman perched on a bench on a patch of grass near to the entrance.

She was crying.

Despite her being a stranger on a strange planet, being a caring and sentimental soul, he slowly padded toward her...

'Excuse me, miss?' he enquired. 'May I sit down?'

The woman looked up, startled. It was Eleanor Johnson.

'Oh my God!' She exclaimed shakily. 'I did not hear you coming!' she nodded to the side empty space beside her on the bench, and Alexander took this as an invitation to take a seat.

They sat in silence for a few seconds as Eleanor sniffed back tears and wiped her eyes.

'So... what's your name?

'Eleanor, but everybody calls me Ellie.' She replied. 'Yours?'

'Alexander, nice to meet you.' he smiled, feeling less tense.

'You too.' Ellie replied, appearing to cheer up slightly. 'What are you doing in Washington with that British accent?'

'I... uh... I'm here to do a public service.' Alexander instantly regretted the words that had fallen out of his mouth and tried to change the subject. 'You seem upset. Do you want to talk about it? Maybe I could help?'

She stared at him for a moment in consideration.

'Sure. But not here.' She rose to her feet. 'Come with me.'

Alexander cautiously followed his new acquaintance, startled by every road they had to cross, but attempting to conceal his plight as best he could to avoid rousing suspicion. After what seemed like an age, they finally reached their destination: Bay Street Restaurant and Lounge.

Alexander looked around as they entered the bar, many of the seats were empty, but there was lively music playing in the background, and a large bar that swept across the edge of the building with cocktail glasses hanging from rails in the ceiling. Ellie approached the bar, and a friendly, young-looking barmaid greeted them.

'Hi there, may I take your order?' She smiled.

'Yes please!' Ellie sighed heartily. 'It's been a day for sure. I will have an Appletini. Alex?'

He didn't respond.

'Alexander?' she repeated.

'Yes?' he replied, suddenly snapping back into reality.

'What do you want to drink?' She asked.

'Uhh...' He panicked, having never been offered an option other than water or juice of the fruits handpicked from trees. 'I'll have what you're having, please.'

'Sure, wait right here.' Said the waitress, as she reached above her head to select two cocktail glasses, and turned her back to Ellie and Alexander while she prepared their drinks.

The pair sat at a table near the bar, and before long, the barmaid placed their Appletinis on the coasters laid out in front of them.

'Thank you.' Ellie smiled and raised her glass. 'Well, to the end of a shitty day.'

Alexander smiled, and Ellie stared at him again.

'Well, cheers?' She chinked her glass gently against that of her companion, still on the table untouched. He eventually caught on, and took a swig of his drink.

'Why on Earth do you drink this stuff?' He asked, a look of disgust sweeping over his face as the bitter alcohol flooded his taste buds.

Ellie giggled at him, then looked thoughtful as the considered his question.

'To escape reality.' She responded. 'The world can be a horrible place. It's nice to take the pressure off now and then. This stuff helps.'

'What makes the world a horrible place?' Alexander asked, unprepared for what Ellie would reply.

'People, mostly.' She said, taking a gulp of her drink.

'That's what I was taught to believe.' Alexander agreed.

'Who on Earth taught you that? It's not a very common philosophy.' She asked, confused.

'My family at home.' He began, before realising he was about to land himself in trouble.

'Were you raised by extra-terrestrials or something?' She laughed, finishing the last of her drink and standing up. 'I'll get us another.'

Alexander started to relax, realising that Ellie was unsuspecting and friendly, and it appeared that they had some opinions in common. He smiled as she returned to the table with more drinks.

'You still haven't told me why you were upset before?' He prodded.

'Uhh it's my boss.' She groaned. 'I work at NASA and they've made a few… alarming discoveries recently which is proving to be really stressful and my boss, well my boss is just an asshole.'

'Oh… What kind of discovery?' Alexander asked, concealing his extensive knowledge surrounding the matter.

'Well, I'm not supposed to talk about it because if the press catch wind, it'll be global news in minutes and there will be much more pressure on the operation.' She explained. 'That's precisely the last thing we need.'

'It sounds serious. Are you at least close to resolving it?' He prodded.

'Not really. My boss basically wants us to defy science, nature, sense.' Ellie sighed heavily. 'Truth is, it's really scary. I feel like we have a social responsibility to overcome the huge threat we're facing; I just don't know how possible it is.' She took a long swig of her drink.

Alexander began to feel more at ease. Azriel had made it seem as though the arrival of humans was imminent, but it appeared this was not the case at all.

'That's a lot of pressure for a handful of people to cope with, don't you think?' Alexander sympathised.

'Yeah, but it would only get worse if we were to invite more people into the know. It's best we gather all the facts and try to come up with some kind of solution before we do.' She took another long swig of her drink. 'Any way, that's enough about work. You said you were here to do a public service… What might that service be?'

'Oh, it's not that important.' He lied. 'Not as important as what you're doing, by the sound of it.'

'Hm, I think you might be right.' Ellie smiled.

The pair chatted for a while longer before Alexander began to feel dizzy from the appletinis and decided to call it a night. The evening breeze blew cold on his face as he walked back to his lodge, which he had grown rather fond of in the last few weeks.

When he reached his home, he lay on his bed and the room spun around him as the alcohol took hold of his mind. He thought of his family in Calathea, reminiscing about the fishing trips he took with Sebastian and the beach rides he enjoyed with Wilbur. He wished he had achieved more during the weeks he had already spent on Earth, but found comfort in his new friendship with Ellie. Not just because she actually worked at NASA and appeared to be well informed about the Calathea mission, but he felt he had found a like-minded companion and enjoyed her company, despite her alternative upbringing and way of life.

Alexander spent a great deal of time with his new acquaintance in the coming weeks. She was outspoken and somewhat coarse at times, but she was also incredibly kind. She devoted much of her free time to volunteering in animal shelters, paying some much-needed attention to the abandoned creatures residing there, and even reading stories to children in orphanages. Alexander tagged along to her volunteer work on several occasions, and was utterly astounded by the amount of wonderful and selfless people he had encountered.

He had grown up believing that there were no good people on Earth, but it seemed to him that this was not the case at all. The museums Ellie and Alexander visited detailing the history of the black community, world wars and yesterday's influential figures, good and bad, suggested that there has always been a clear distinction between kindness and evil.

Sheer turmoil evoked by all he had witnessed alongside Ellie wrecked any certainty he ever had surrounding the merit of his mission.

It was obvious to him that among the evil embodied by many members of the human race, there was good. Much good. Devotion to righting the wrongs of yesterday in the hope of forging a better tomorrow.

The kindness of the people working with abused animals allowed them to love and trust humanity again, as if that trust had never been broken. He thought that a valuable lesson could be learned by an animal's ability to discard the memories of treachery, to simply have faith in the fact that those that prove themselves can be relied upon to see that they never have to suffer again.

He wondered if those attempting to reverse the wrongdoing of their neighbours, should also be forced the reap the consequences.

Something Ellie had said to him sent a wave of guilt through his stomach.

'You reap what you sow in this world.'

Her words echoed in his mind.

He considered whether that was actually true.

Sometimes those who sow nothing but kindness, are left to reap the consequences of those who do not conduct themselves so honourably.

Why should this reality come to fruition at his hands, allowing the end of the world to engulf not just those who deserve it, but also those who do not deserve it at all?

Chapter 7 – Arousing Suspicion

'It's been weeks, Azriel.' His wife said sternly. 'We ought to check on him. What if he's come to grief?'

'My love.' He placed his hands on her tensed shoulders, speaking softly in an attempt to calm her. 'We haven't just sent him fishing. He's gone to Earth to ensure the future safety of our new home, to serve the supreme being that is Anad. He was never going to be there and back in a day.'

Althea stared at the ground.

'He'll be back before you know it.' Azriel kissed her forehead.

'Don't you worry about your boy, Althea.' Sebastian instructed her, noticing the tender moment between the parents. 'If our fishing trips taught him anything, it's how to survive.' He teased.

Althea rolled her eyes and giggled.

'Do I want to know what you and my son got up to when you'd disappear for hours, Sebastian?'

'Hmm... I very much doubt it!' He winked playfully and threw his arm around her. 'He's a wise young man, Althea. Trust him.' He patted her shoulder and followed Azriel to the forest to fetch firewood.

Completely unaware that his mother was sick with worry, Alexander awoke to find the sun beaming cheerfully on the beautiful nature around him. He decided to take a long walk and explore the area even further than he had already. Dressing himself in a soft pink polo shirt and black denim shorts, he threw his front door open, and triumphantly strolled through the trees toward civilisation. Today, he felt as confident as he ever had on Earth.

As he wandered the streets of Washington, he exchanged smiles with strangers as he did in Calathea, and observed the innocent nature nestling in trees and hedges, noticeably more frightened of him here than at home.

His soaring spirits were dampened once more by the sickening realisation that Earth would soon cease to exist, and its inhabitants were condemned to perish with it. He tried to tell himself that it was inevitable, with or without his interventions, the fateful day would come, and even the most sentient of beings would be powerless to stop it. He wondered whether humankind should be given a second chance, a fresh start, an opportunity to repent their wrongdoing and learn to live as Omniscients do; with consideration for every creature in all that they do.

He noticed a puppy and a young child playing gleefully on a patch of grass nearby, and he thought of himself as a child with Wilbur. Why shouldn't they be given the chance to prosper?

The innocence of youth allows a greater perspective to be embraced by impressionable minds. The sins of mature humankind need not be paid for by the young, and certainly not those which suffer most at the hands of humanity. Nature.

Alexander found his mind running away with him as he battled with his conscience and the brush with which he had been taught to tarnish all mankind. His observations over the past weeks had brought him to some personal conclusions.

It seemed to him that humanity was a vast collection of different beliefs and attitudes. The burden of responsibility appeared to weigh heavier on some human minds than it did on others. Unfortunately, those that feel the woes of the world most keenly, least have means to rectify them, while those burdened only by their lust for power take precedence.

'Is ending an entire species the right way to reprimand the less enlightened members?' He whispered to himself.

He struggled to comprehend his own question, as he considered the many years of observation Anad endured. He must have considered this question himself, at some stage. He recalled the atrocious events his Omniscient fellows had been selected to remedy, long before his existence. The inflections in his eyes emulated that of his father and began to spin. They transported his mind to the very places that had been described to him, witnessing the cruelty of humanity.

They never seemed to learn their lesson as the previous species did. Will it ever be possible for such psychologically complex beings to live harmoniously while their views and opinions remain so-

'Oh!' Ellie exclaimed as Alexander's body collided with hers. His mind was elsewhere entirely. 'Alex?'

His eyes appeared to focus as he regained consciousness.

'Ellie!' He gasped, startled as his mind joined his body where he stood. 'I'm so sorry I-I was-.'

'On another planet by the looks!' She joked. 'What's up? I haven't seen you for a while.'

'I, yeah, I've just been-.' Struggling to redirect his thoughts, he began to panic, tripping over his tongue.

'Come sit down you look like you need a minute.' She grabbed his hand and dragged him toward a picnic blanket in the middle of the crowded, grassy park they found themselves in.

Ellie lay back on the picnic blanket and closed her eyes. Alexander sat beside her, slightly uncomfortable.

'What's happened, Alex?' Ellie asked, sensing his awkwardness. 'You seem very on edge.'

'Nothing has happened I've just been... Thinking about things.' He answered honestly.

'What things?'

'It's just that, no matter what the "right thing" might seem to be, there always has to be someone that suffers.' He almost whispered, profoundly.

Ellie sat up and a sympathetic expression swept across her face.

'That's exactly what this thing at work is about.' She sighed. 'How can it be that one group of people that have declared themselves as "superior" get to play God and make decisions that have the potential to cost lives. Not just people but other beings, too.'

Relaxing slightly, Alexander lay back on the picnic blanket.

'All we can do is what we think is right.' He suggested.

'It's not always that simple.' Ellie disagreed. 'We're often not permitted to do what we think is right. There are too many people with too many opinions.'

'What does your job actually involve? It all sounds very serious.' Alexander prodded, hoping to gather some information as to the mission he was pretending to know nothing about.

'Well, that is a good question.' Ellie perked up, obviously passionate about her occupation. 'I am the head of the Earth Observatory department for NASA, and we explore the Earth's course in the solar system, the climate, Earth's history and share this information with the world.'

'That sounds very interesting. What kind of things do you find out about Earth's history?' Alexander asked.

'Basically, when it was formed, when it was hit by asteroids, how the atmosphere has changed to accommodate human life, to name just a few. It's truly fascinating.' Ellie explained.

'Do you think there is life on other planets?' Alexander's heart rate increased as he began to tread in dangerous territory, hoping that Ellie would slip up and divulge the status of the Calathea mission.

'Absolutely. That's the main reason I got into this job. I've always been so interested in discovering what's out there. There is so much to uncover beyond our planet and it's becoming increasingly apparent that there are species very similar to us out there. I'd love to know how they live, if they do things in a similar way to us, or if they do things… Better.'

Ellie's eyes twinkled with excitement as she spoke. Alexander was mesmerised by her ambition and desire. She was certainly nothing like the humans his parents had described to him.

'Do you think you'll ever visit another planet?' Alexander held his breath.

'I would love to. Recently it seems more possible than ever, with this new discovery we've made.' Ellie looked at him without turning her head, realising she had perhaps said too much.

'Is there another place suitable for human life?' He asked anxiously.

'Potentially… I really can't say, we know very little at this point.' She grappled for a new topic of conversation. 'Can I show you something later? Just somewhere I go when things get too much.'

'Yeah.' Alexander smiled. 'I'd like that.'

'Cool, meet me here at nightfall.'

Soon enough, darkness consumed the city and Alex made for the park once more. He struggled to find his way back as he was so distracted by his thoughts when he first made the trip that morning he wasn't concentrating on the directions.

The streetlights guided his path towards Ellie, who was already waiting for him with a smile.

'Hey.' She smiled, handing him a plastic bag containing a liquid he had never heard of. 'I gotta grab a few things from my apartment before we go, why don't you come up with me and wait?'

Alexander smiled and nodded.

They approached the apartment building, a tall, glassy structure with trees planted inside slate squares dotted along the pavement outside the revolving door.

Ellie typed her pin number into the keypad beside the door, and it began to spin, allowing them entrance to the lobby. Inside, was a large, black marble desk manned by a cheery, older lady with blonde curls striped with the odd grey streak.

'Hey, Ellie!' She called over the top of her computer as she always did when Ellie and Chelsea arrived home.

'Hey, Linda!' She replied as the doors of the lift opened.

They reached the sixth floor and approached apartment number 603. Ellie entered first, holding the door for Alexander. Once inside, they discovered that they were not alone. Ellie's roommate, Chelsea, was stood in the kitchen. A medium height young lady with an hourglass figure, auburn hair and big, brown eyes that smiled with her cheeks.

'This must be Alex!' Chelsea teased, grabbing Ellie's arm. 'Great to meet you! I've heard so much about you!'

Alexander looked concerned.

'All good, don't worry!' She squeaked in her high-pitched voice. 'I'm Chelsea.'

'Nice to meet you, Chelsea.' Alexander shook her hand.

'We're just here to grab a few things, then we're going to the rooftop.' Ellie explained.

'I see!' Chelsea winked at her roommate, who shot her a glare. 'Should I make myself scarce?'

'No, no that's not necessary.' Ellie widened her eyes at Chelsea and raised her eyebrows.

'Seriously, I don't wanna-'

'-Really, Chelsea. You can hang out. I'm just gonna grab a few things then we're gonna head out. You two wait in here.' Ellie called as she disappeared into her bedroom, leaving Chelsea and Alexander alone.

Alexander milled slightly awkwardly around the kitchen table as Chelsea buzzed around.

'Sit down, Alex.' She smiled as she floated around him, putting clean crockery and cutlery away in various places. 'Tell me about yourself.'

'Well...' He scrambled as there were few things he could actually tell her about himself. 'There's not much to tell. I am an only child. Tell me about yourself instead.' He quickly changed the subject.

'I am also an only child.' She began. 'I grew up in a city not far from here and I'm a police officer.'

'That's very interesting.' Alexander replied earnestly. 'What exactly does your job entail?'

'All kinds of horrible things! I see a lot of crimes like child abuse and animal abuse.' Chelsea answered. 'Knife crime.'

There was a brief silence.

'Why did you decide to work with the police, Chelsea?' Alexander asked.

'A number of reasons.' She sat down opposite him. 'To give something back to the community, keep people safe, but mainly because my dad was killed fifteen years ago, and they never caught the guys responsible.'

'I'm so sorry.' Alexander smiled sympathetically.

Chelsea smiled half-heartedly and nodded as if to thank him for his condolences.

'It's actually his birthday tomorrow.' Chelsea continued. 'He was very interested in war, so Ellie and I are going to listen to a Holocaust survivor speak in town to mark the occasion. You should come along! Are you interested in war?'

'I am, I'm very interested in history.' He replied enthusiastically. 'Ellie and I have visited a few museums together since I got here.'

Alexander's interest in Chelsea's profession and history of the events his Omniscient family had witnessed distracted him from pursuing his investigation with Ellie, but provided a useful cover to avoid arousing suspicion.

'Great! She's speaking at the town hall a few blocks away at 8pm on Friday night.'

Ellie emerged from her bedroom holding a rucksack.

'Ready to go?' She asked Alexander.

'Let's go.' He replied, standing up. 'Nice to meet you, Chelsea!'

'You, too! See you Friday!' Chelsea replied happily.

'Friday?' Ellie looked confused.

'Yeah, I invited him to come to the town hall with us.' She grinned cheekily at her roommate.

'Whatever, see ya later, Chelsea.' Ellie ushered Alexander to the door, and shot Chelsea a backward glance as they exited the apartment.

She led the way toward a very tall hotel building a few blocks away, and they climbed until they reached the deserted rooftop. From there, they could see all the illuminated buildings that surrounded, glimmering in the darkness. Alexander stared about his surroundings in awe, while Ellie laid out a quilted mat for them to lie on, with some pillows to rest their heads.

She handed Alexander two plastic tumblers and poured them each a large Zinfandel.

'What's this?' Alexander asked.

'It's a… Californian Zinfandel.' Ellie read off the label as she screwed the lid back on, unaware that he had never seen a bottle of wine before.

She took a tumbler from his hand and lay back on the blanket, Alex followed suit and lay beside her.

'Wow!' He exclaimed, as the constellations of stars sparkled brilliantly in the sky above him. 'Is this what you wanted to show me?'

'Yeah, it's pretty cool up here.' Ellie smiled. 'Look through this.' She instructed, passing him a handheld telescope, before taking a large gulp of wine.

Completely enchanted by the magnified stars, Alex stared through the telescope, muttering to himself. Ellie watched, heart warmed by his sheer innocence and obvious purity of heart.

After a few minutes, he noticed something different through the telescope, it didn't look like all the other stars he had been looking at, so he decided to consult the expert.

'Look at this, Ellie.' He handed the telescope to her and pointed in the direction of the unusual structure. 'What's that?'

She peered attentively through the telescope and examined the sky for a short while.

'That is a planet.' She began. 'It's much nearer to Earth than any others, and as far as we know it has only recently formed. It has puzzled NASA for a while now as we hadn't detected any asteroids at risk of colliding to form a planet-like structure.' She furrowed her brow. 'It's almost… supernatural.'

Alexander's stomach tightened as he realised he had spotted his home, Calathea. Ellie put down the telescope and finished her wine, before topping up both of their tumblers.

'Maybe it is.' He began, dangerously unaccustomed to the effects of alcohol, he found himself firmly in its grasp, losing control of his inhibitions. 'Who knows what's going on beyond the Earth.'

'Do you know something I don't?' Ellie asked, half joking, half suspicious.

'No, no. I, I just meant that-'

'I'm starting to think there is more to you than meets the eye, Alex.' She brushed her fingertips across the back of his hand. 'You're a mystery. Who are you?' Her voice trailed into a seductive whisper as she traced his skin.

'Well, I'm...' His breathing quickened as Ellie sat up and looked deep into his eyes, as he lay beneath her gaze. Her hands deviated further up his arm, sending tingles down his spine.

She kissed him softly and his heart raced. The troubles that plagued him earlier melted away as he found himself existing entirely in that moment.

There was no yesterday, no tomorrow. Just now.

She ran her fingers up his arm and stroked his neck as they shared a long, romantic kiss. Alexander, inexperienced as he was, didn't know what to do with his hands, but found himself following Ellie's lead.

She was revealing herself to be the domineering type. Knows exactly what she wants, even more certain of how to get it. She caressed his cheek as their kiss came to an end, and she smiled sweetly at Alexander.

'What's this?' Ellie asked, fingering his necklace.

'My Uncle Sebastian gave it to me when I was a child.' Alexander answered.

'Do you ever take it off?'

'Never.' He smiled, placing his fingers over hers as she continued to touch the pendant.

They continued to sip at their drinks until late in the evening when it grew too cold to sit outside, and they left the rooftop.

When they reached the street, Alexander noticed an elaborately dressed young man being harassed by a pair of inebriated young males. He was wearing a bright blonde wig, pastel pink, shiny boots that reached just below his knees with fishnet tights, a white, frilly skirt and tube top, complemented by a light purple feather coat.

'What are you supposed to be, puff?' Slurred one of them, tugging at the feathers on his coat, ripping them out and throwing them in the face of the young man.

Black, mascara filled tears rolled down his cheek, carving a pain-filled tramline in the pink blush, past his deep pink lips, overlined by a black lip liner.

The other man threw dollar bills in his face and yelled 'cheap man whore', spit flying from his monstrous mouth.

Alcohol and outrage cursing through his veins, Alexander lunged forward to offer his assistance when Ellie gripped his arm and pulled him back.

'No, Alex!' She exclaimed. 'It's too dangerous, you never know what these people are capable of.'

'Who else is going to help him?' He shouted, astonished that she was prepared to do nothing. 'If one man refuses to protect another what hope is there?'

He marched straight into the centre of the chaos and positioned himself between the young man and his tormentors.

'Perhaps you can clarify something for me, why do you deem yourself so above this man that you have the right to ridicule him in this way?' He stared straight into the eyes of the man stood before him and awaited his answer. Meanwhile the drag queen took advantage of the distraction by fleeing the scene.

They laughed at Alexander and took a step forward so as to intimidate him.

'What's it to you, English boy?' One of them asked menacingly. 'Are you a puff as well? Wanted to be his hero so he'd suck your cock?'

'Alex, it's time to go.' Ellie said sternly, running over and pulling him away from the two boys.

'No, he wants her to suck his cock.' They laughed like hysterical hyenas. 'Playing the hero so *she'll* get on her knees. Well, how about you suck my cock instead?' He grabbed her ponytail and threw her to the floor, her knees bashing the concrete with a painful thump.

The red mist descended, and Alexander's rage exploded. He stepped in front of Ellie, struggling to her feet, knees bleeding. He pushed the arrogant young peer to the ground. Astonished by his strength, he leapt from the floor and drove his fist into the centre of Alexander's face, who caught his hand and threw him back with such force he smacked into a 'trash can' on the other side of the street, creating a terrible commotion.

Ellie spectated in a state of sheer amazement, as the perplexed thugs continued to target Alexander.

As they strutted back toward him, he clicked his fingers and an intense breeze separated the two abusers from Alexander and Ellie.

'How the hell are you doing that, Alex?' Ellie asked suspiciously, after a few seconds of deafening silence.

He turned to look at her puzzled, frightened expression before realising he had just exposed himself as being 'different'. With the click of his fingers, the breeze calmed and the thugs charged at him.

A metallic flash shone in his eyes before a sharp pain surged through his body like an earthquake sending shockwaves from its epicentre. The two boys turned and ran into the night, leaving Ellie and Alexander in the middle of the street. As they retreated, a loud clank echoed through the empty space, and blood began to gush from the centre of Alexander's ribcage.

He had been stabbed.

'No, Alex!' Ellie screamed tearfully, catching him as he fell to the ground in agony. She desperately tried to stem the flow of blood now pouring from the wound, ripping the sleeve off of his shirt and pressing it to his chest.

With blood-stained hands, she fished through her pockets to find her phone and dialled 911. When the ambulance arrived, the paramedic jumped out and Ellie sighed with relief.

'Please don't let him die!' She blubbered.

'Does he have insurance?' The paramedic asked, staring sternly at Ellie, disregarding the critical state Alexander was in.

'Fuck you.' Ellie grunted in his face, disgusted, before throwing his first aid kit at him and ordering him to show some humanity and help the dying man on the floor, his breathing stiffening with every second that ticked by.

A second paramedic wheeled a stretcher out of the ambulance, and they carefully lifted Alexander's lifeless carcass on to it. They removed his necklace and handed it to Ellie.

Alexander drifted in and out of consciousness as the paramedics wheeled him through the hospital corridors. He heard the muffled cries of nurses using medical terms he had never heard before, and Ellie begging them not to let him die.

'He needs to get to theatre now, get Dr Ratesh and Dr Simmonds, they're on call tonight. He'll need a blood transfusion; we think he's lost about 12 pints of blood. Who has his medical records, please? I need to check his blood type.' Directed Nurse Miller.

'We can't find any medical records for him, his name is Alexander and that's all we know about him.' Replied the paramedic.

'How strange. No time to waste, test his blood and fast track the results so we can get him what he needs. Richards, prep for theatre.' Miller brushed off the abnormality surrounding her patient and continued with her duties.

Now in theatre, Alexander was placed under general anaesthetic and the doctors began to explore the stab wound.

'Scalpel.' Dr Ratesh requested, holding out his left hand. 'We'll need to check for punctures to the heart and the lungs, the wound is located to the left of the mediastinum so there is a huge risk that the knife made contact.'

As he made an incision to get a better look at the damage, he noticed the heart beating beneath Alexander's chest was not white, tinted red by blood, but gold. In utter amazement, all Dr Ratesh and Dr Simmonds could do, was simply stare at each other.

He made a further incision in Alex's skin, to reveal his golden heart, and at that moment, Nurse Miller entered, concerned that there was an unidentified substance present in his blood stream.

'High levels of alcohol, and a substance I have never encountered in all my years of examining blood test results.' Miller explained. 'A new legal high, do we think?'

'No.' Dr Ratesh answered matter-of-factly, the colour draining from his face, his voice muffled by the mask concealing his breath. 'Whoever this is… he isn't human.'

Chapter 8 – Dancing Monkey

'For the last time, I have only known him for a few weeks. He said he was here on a public errand or something... All I know about him is he is very high principled, and his name is Alex.' Ellie told the police officer Randle interrogating her, while Alexander recovered from his major surgery.

'Very well, Miss Johnson. Thank you for your time.' He responded, closing his notepad, and tucking it into his pocket.

Alexander blinked frantically as he began to regain consciousness and he adjusted to the bright lights in the hospital. He lifted his right hand to rub his stinging eyes and realised it was being restrained by something.

He was handcuffed to the bed.

He stared about the room and noticed police armed with rifles guarding the door, and a nervous looking Ellie at his bedside.

'Ellie, what happened to me?' He croaked, panic stricken. 'What's going on?'

'Who are you, Alex?' She stood over him and spoke sternly.

'You know who I am, I'm-'

'WHO ARE YOU, ALEX?' She wailed, tears welling up in her eyes. 'WHAT PUBLIC SERVICE, WHERE DID YOU COME FROM, HOW DID YOU MAKE THAT WIND?' Her wild eyes remained fixed on his, as his befuddled brain attempted to scrape a convincing lie together.

He stuttered and stammered, desperate to cling to the delusion that he was no imposter, but alas, his brain wouldn't let him.

'I can't tell you. I'm sorry, Ellie.' Alexander looked away, unable to withstand the intense glare from her.

She shook her head, and a single tear fell from her eye and rolled down her cheek, falling with her spirits.

'I wanna leave.' She stormed to the door and stood before officer Wilkins guarding it. Without a backward glance or another word, she left.

'Get the doctor.' Wilkins told Randle.

A few minutes later, the police officer returned with Dr Ratesh.

'Good afternoon, sir.' He began. 'How are you feeling, first?'

'Strange.' Alexander replied. 'Very strange.'

'Yes. It certainly seems that way.' Dr Ratesh's tone darkened. 'Alexander there are no records whatsoever that you actually exist, you have inhumane features and no medical insurance. We are struggling to understand where you came from, would you care to explain?'

'I'm not sure I can.' Alexander replied, without making eye contact with the doctor. The gravity of the situation began to dawn on him, and he scrambled to get out of there.

Though desperately trying to free himself from the shackles that restrained him, the anaesthetic coursing through his veins capped his strength and Omniscient influence, and he worked himself into a frenzy of sheer panic.

'Please, undo these I can't-' he gasped, rattling the rail that he was handcuffed to.

Dr Ratesh stood over him, watching him squirm as if he were a winged pheasant struggling before a hunter saw fit to finish the job. He caught his flailing left arm and gripped it tightly, stabbing his skin with a needle and injected a sedative into his vein; the scrambling ceased as the drug took hold of his limbs.

He was completely powerless to protect himself from the suspicious doctor.

A loud, engine like sound and a blinding light woke him from his artificial sleep. He used all the strength he could muster to try and sit up, and was confronted with a hard roof that made a sickening crack when it connected with his head. This time, both his arms and his legs were restrained. Through squinted eyes, he observed that he was in an enclosed dome. Why he was in there however, he could not say.

After what seemed like an age, the noise quietened, the light dimmed, and he slowly exited the narrow dome that encapsulated him. The cold light of day revealed several doctors, including Ratesh and Miller, gathered around a screen and discussing the images it displayed. A short while of nodding and pointing and debating led to the doctors silently entering the room Alexander occupied. They handled him harshly, like a piece of raw meat tossed onto a chopping board and flicked around like an object without sense or humanity.

He was wheeled into a different room, lifted from the bed and dropped onto a cold, metal chair, where all manner of wires and intimidating looking equipment was attached to the skin of his chest and forehead. He dared not put up a fight for fear that he would again be injected with the substance unbeknown to him, which stripped him of his senses and of his dignity.

Once the doctors had finished decorating him like a Christmas tree, they presented him with a series of tests, forcing him to undertake to complete tasks which began with simple copying exercises of shapes and patterns, graduating to questions about humans as a species, important historical events, and other subjects. During this time, they drew blood samples, DNA samples and injected him with hormones to test their effect on his body, assuming he was inhuman. Holding his head back by his hair, they shone lights in his eyes and photographed his face, plastered with a defeated expression.

After several hours of being tested and tortured, a man named Christian Evernaut entered the room, and sat in the chair opposite him. A British man, with white, wiry hair and wild, ungroomed eyebrows. His grey eyes were kind, and his skin wrinkled. He held a hard back notepad, black in colour, and a pen decorated with an 'Evernaut Psychology' logo.

He appeared to be examining a document and scribbling some brief notes, before he finally addressed the barely clothed man shivering before him, his knuckles white from gripping the arm rest of his chair, his arms bruised by needles.

'Good afternoon, Alexander.' Evernaut began, calmly. 'My name is Dr Christian Evernaut. I am a psychologist. The Police and Doctors of this city have expressed concerns pertaining to your apparent abnormality, relating to the differences in your brain structure, and certain features beneath your skin. I am here to discuss these abnormalities with you.'

Alexander remained silent, but glared straight into the psychologist's eyes, with a strong and stern expression painted on to his face, concealing his fear and exhaustion.

'I understand that you sustained an injury at the hands of two young men two nights ago, whereby you were stabbed with a knife near your mediastinum, and were brought in for treatment to your wound as a result.' He paused for a moment. 'Is this correct, Alexander?'

Alexander nodded once, maintaining piercing eye contact with the psychologist.

'The surgeons performing your surgery, Dr Ratesh and Dr Miller discovered that your heart is gold in colour. I'm sure you are aware that this is abnormal for homo sapiens, and wonder if you might tell me a bit about where you came from?' Evernaut continued, his pen poised to his pad.

Before he spoke, Alexander examined the machine that the wires taped to his chest were hooked up to. It seemed to be creating lines consistent with his breathing pattern, and he knew he had to remain as calm as he possibly could.

There was a long pause as he gathered his thoughts.

'I am a human with a... somewhat heightened sense of awareness.' He said carefully, monitoring the lines that appeared as he spoke.

'What do you think has influenced this "heightened sense of awareness"?' Evernaut asked.

'My perspective.' Alexander replied instantly.

The spikes on the screen remained level, and the room was silent, aside from Evernaut's pen scratching on the page upon which he was writing.

'This morning the Doctors performed a CT scan and an MRI scan on your brain to examine the structure and activity.' He explained, with several gestures of the hand. 'The results they obtained from these tests displayed such that have never been found in recorded medical history. This, combined with the abnormalities found with your heart, has led us to believe that you do not belong to the homo sapiens species. What do you have to say about this?'

Alexander thought carefully.

'Have these doctors conducted a "CT scan" on every member of the "homo sapiens species", sir?'

'No, sir.' Evernaut answered, half laughing. 'I'm sure you can appreciate that it would be entirely impractical to conduct unnecessary CT scans on every member of the-'

'In that case, Christian,' Alexander continued, leaning forward slightly as his confidence grew. 'How can you be sure that there *are* no other homo sapiens with the same brain structure and activity as mine?'

'Well-'

'Have Dr Miller and Dr Ratesh sliced open every man in history to check their heart is the same as every other one they have seen before?' He interrupted.

'Alexander-'

As the feeling of timidness was replaced with a white-hot rage whirring in his mind, Alexander sprang from the uncomfortable metal chair, flinging the machine he was wired to across the room and ripping the tape off his chest and head. Noticing the camera he had been photographed by, he picked it up and smashed it, destroying any hope of identifying him if he escaped the clutches of the doctors.

'I will not answer any more questions.' He declared firmly. 'I would like to leave.'

Alexander marched toward the door, the adrenaline raging through his veins distracted him from the searing pain of his freshly sewn stab wound, and the inflections in his iris' were expanding and contracting very obviously. Azriel's began to do the same, all the way from Calathea. At that moment, he too was staring into Evernaut's eyes.

Christian leapt up from his seat and blocked the door with his body. Noticing yet another unusual feature of Alexander's, he drew a needle from his pocket and tried to sedate his patient. Unencumbered by anaesthetic, his strength outweighed that of his opponent, and snatched the needle from the psychologist, snapping it with one hand. He stared into Christian's eyes intensely.

'No thank you, Doctor. Excuse me.' He requested placidly.

After a few thoughtful moments, he admitted defeat and stood aside.

'Althea, I think something is wrong.' Azriel called to his wife.

Alexander dashed around the maze of hospital corridors.

'What's going on?' Althea half whispered, the colour draining from her face.

With every suspicious doctor he passed, a locked door impeded his progress.

'He's in a hospital.' Azriel observed, blind to his own surroundings as his vision connected with that of his son.

Impatient to leave, he hauled the nearest window open and swung his body through it, ripping one of his stitches as his skin stretched.

'What's he doing in a hospital?' Althea asked, monotonal and frozen with fear.

Dr Miller spotted him and ran to the window, screaming 'SUICIDE!'

'He's hurt.' Azriel confirmed.

Alexander clicked his fingers and floated to the ground.

Then he ran.

Blood pouring from his wound. Beads of sweat pouring from his brow. His troublesome, golden heart slamming against his ribs.

'WE HAVE GOT TO DO SOMETHING!' Althea screamed, tugging at Azriel's clothes, tears streaming from her sheet-white face. People emerged from all over to see what the commotion was about.

Alexander groaned as he ran, the adrenaline no longer numbing his pain.

A billboard up ahead read:

'ALIENS IN AMERICA?

Man in a human body with inhuman features undergoing tests in Washington Hospital.'

William Hickory slammed a newspaper article on to Eleanor Johnson's desk, and the penny dropped in her brain:

Extra-Terrestrials On Earth?

Washington surgeons operating on a 'man' stabbed in the chest earlier this week made a shocking discovery when checking for lung and heart damage, found that he takes the phrase 'heart of gold' to a new extreme.

His heart is, literally, gold.

When conducting CT and MRI scans, the results showed brain structure and activity never previously identified in a human, as well as an unidentified substance present in his blood stream.

New legal high, or new species of human?

The Doctors treating the patient said:

'It was complete shock. We have never seen anything like it. He does not match the Homo Sapiens criteria and has no medical records to suggest he ever existed as a citizen on this planet.'

This discovery comes with leaked information from NASA of a mystery new planet that has appeared in the solar system, considerably closer to Earth than any other planet. NASA officials are yet to comment on these rumours.

'Prepare your team to send a rocket to our mystery planet.' He ordered, with a smirk.

Chapter 9 – A Great Escape

Alexander stumbled through the door of his home, certain that he couldn't run any further.

He slammed the door behind him, resting his head against it with his eyes closed, breathing loudly and heavily, desperate to catch his breath.

He looked down at his clothes to find them soaked with blood that was now collecting at his feet as it fell from his chest.

'Great.' He spat as it dawned on him that his mother and her healing hands were not there to remedy his wounds.

He fell into the chair closest to him and removed the bandage around his chest to reveal the open wound with stitches hanging out of it. He grabbed a tea towel from across the table and pressed it to his chest, gasping in pain.

His head was thudding and his vision was blurred. He hadn't yet caught his breath and he couldn't think straight.

He tried to take deep breaths, but his frantic heartbeat unsettled him. He struggled to compose himself.

The bleeding, the breathlessness, he'd completely exposed himself to humankind, and he remembered what Ellie said about big news spreading like wildfire across the globe.

He was right to be concerned.

All over the world, astounded news reporters shared his story, rather like Chinese whispers, each reporter adding a sprinkle of drama to the reality to make for more exciting listening than the last.

For now, however, his greatest concern was stemming the leakage of his precious blood from his wound.

He took a deep breath through his nose and blew it from his mouth.

'Ok,' he whispered breathlessly to himself. 'You can do this.'

He closed his hand tightly around the tea towel in his hand, and it compacted into a tightly wrapped bandage. He slowly rose to his feet, one hand on the table for balance, the other on his wound, and plucked a needle from a drawer in his bed side table.

Closing his eyes and taking another deep breath, he threaded the end of his broken stitch through his needle and pierced the edge of his wound with its painfully sharp point.

Groaning in agony and through gritted teeth, he sewed his own stitches back up. Once his skin was fastened back together, he bound his chest and sat, head in hands, contemplating what in the world he was going to do next.

Despite his exhaustion from being poked, prodded and examined and running for his life, Alexander could not sleep.

He thought of his mother and his father. He wondered if they knew what had happened to him, if they were going to do something to help him.

He also thought of Ellie. He felt guilty for being dishonest, he felt terrible that if he executed his mission successfully, she would also fall victim to the outcome.

Ellie thought of him, too.

She wondered where he was hiding, if he was recovering from his attack and his surgery, but most of all, she wondered who he was. Before these shocking discoveries, she thought he was a kind, honest and sweet young man with a big heart and good intentions.

'A heart of gold, you might say.' Ellie sniggered as she lay, fully clothed on her bed. 'The irony is just fantastic.'

She held his necklace in her hands.

Her bedroom was messy, with white walls and grey blinds covering her window. She had a black desk with a matching chair and lamp, strewn with papers and books in an organised chaos, symbolic of the state of her mind.

As she revisited all the conversations she had with Alexander, she recalled how interested he was in her job, the subtle prods that she thought nothing of at the time, that now seemed suspicious.

'Do you think there's life on other planets?' 'Is there another place suitable for human life?'

A ripple of realisation surged through Ellie's very being.

He didn't *want* to know if there was life on other planets, he already *knew* that. He wanted to know if she knew. If the world knew.

One thing was clear to her, she had to find him. He could be detrimental to their mission to discover their mystery planet.

Her thoughts were disturbed by her roommate, Chelsea, a police officer, entering their apartment and slamming the front door behind her.

'Ell?' She shouted from the kitchen, her footsteps getting closer. 'Have you seen this?'

Ellie joined her in the kitchen, where she stood holding a brown paper bag filled with groceries in her left hand, and her phone in her right. She placed it on the table and gestured for Ellie to look at the illuminated screen.

It was the same news article that William Hickory had slammed on her desk earlier that day.

'Yes, I've seen it, Chels.' She said, miserably.

Chelsea raised her eyebrow and jerked her head to the left.

'What's up with you? Isn't this good? Doesn't this help your new mission at work? It'll definitely make my job a lot more interesting!' She rambled, shocked by Ellie's dejectedness.

'Yes, it could help.' Ellie agreed. 'Enormously.'

'But...?' Chelsea nodded slowly and turned her wrist in a circular motion, encouraging her roommate to continue.

Ellie sighed.

'You remember that guy... Alex?' She began, reluctantly.

'Don't tell me it's him?' Chelsea dropped her bag of groceries on the table, her eyes wide.

'It's him, ok?' Ellie snapped, sinking into a chair and planting her face into her hands. 'When he was stabbed, he was protecting me from some assholes terrorising Eddie Fairstone, you know the drag queen, 'Pastel Princess'?'

Chelsea nodded slowly.

'So, this really sweet guy that you have been hanging out with and clearly gives a shit about you, that could help you with this huge mission that's been stressing you out for months, is a cause to sit there with a face like a slapped ass?'

'He wouldn't tell me who he is or where he's from.' Ellie replied sharply. 'He won't help me, Chelsea. He'll only make it worse.'

'You're being stubborn.' Chelsea clapped back. 'You've just got your panties in a bunch because your boss is a dick and there's more to your new boyfriend than you thought there was.'

'I haven't got my-'

'Did you even give him a shot at explaining everything to you?' Chelsea interrupted. 'Or did you just scream in his face and run off like you always do?'

Ellie was silent.

Chelsea raised both eyebrows at her.

'WELL?' She jabbed, as Ellie tried to ignore her and return to her bedroom, proving her point.

'YES, CHELSEA.' Ellie yelled across the room, tears filling her sad eyes. 'I screamed in his face and I left him there in a hospital full of armed cops and doctors that were just gonna poke him and prod him and treat him like a piece of garbage.' Her voice trailed out with her cries and Chelsea placed a consoling hand on her shoulder.

'You know what you have to do, don't you?' She asked softly.

'Yes.' Ellie sniffed. 'I have to go find him.'

The next morning, Ellie did just that. She vaguely remembered the direction that he had come from when they met on that fateful night. She padded across the park toward the break in the hedge running alongside the pavement. Beyond the concrete was grass and a well-trodden trail into the trees, where Alexander had made his home. She walked deep into the forestry and came across a structure she had never seen there before. In the window, she saw Alexander, topless, blood seeping through the bandage he had bound his chest with the night before.

She burst through his front door, startling him beyond belief. They stared at one another for a few moments, tears spilling from Ellie's eyes as she caught sight of the bruises dotted along his arms, evidence of the abuse he had been subjected to. She couldn't even look at his stab wound.

The stab wound he had obtained protecting her.

'I didn't expect to see you again.' Alexander broke the excruciating silence, speaking grittily.

'I wanted to apologise.' She said shakily. 'I never really gave you a chance to explain yourself.'

'Ellie-'

'Let me help you with this.' Ellie deflected Alexander's inevitable excuses. 'You must be in a lot of pain.'

She gently removed the bandage concealing his horrific wound, blood still oozing slowly from the stitches Alexander had sewn back into his own skin.

'Sit here.' She pulled out the chair he had sat in the night before, and routed through her bag to reveal an antiseptic solution and cotton balls. 'This might sting a little bit.'

Ellie pressed a soaked cotton ball onto the blood-stained area in the centre of his chest. Alexander inhaled sharply through his clamped jaw. She cleaned the wound and redressed it with a fresh bandage she removed from her bag.

'Thank you, Ellie.' Alexander said genuinely.

'What did they do to you?' Ellie asked, running her fingers gently along the many small, purple bruises across both of his arms.

'They tested me.' The usual sparkle in his eyes was now dull and hopeless.

'I should never have left you there.' Ellie whispered tearily. 'I guess it was just a shock... It's not every day that you...'

'Ellie.' Alexander gripped both of her hands to stop her from tracing his bruised arms. 'I understand why you're upset. I haven't been completely honest with you, but I also haven't lied. My name is Alexander, and I am here to do a public service, I just can't tell you what it is. Much like you can't tell me what this huge discovery you have made at work is all about.'

'I think you know *exactly* what it's about.' Ellie responded immediately. 'That's another reason I wanted to come find you.'

Alexander stared blankly into Ellie's eyes, backed into a corner.

'Tell me what you know about my situation at work.' Ellie demanded.

Alexander continued to stare at her, considering his position.

'I know that you've discovered a new planet that you deem to be suitable to sustain human life. I also know that this discovery comes at a very convenient time, given that the Earth's course has mysteriously changed and is now rapidly approaching the sun, considerably sooner than expected. I know that your boss wants to send humans there.' He already regretted the words that rolled off his tongue.

'What do you know about this planet? How do you know all this?'

Alexander was silent.

'Alex?'

At that moment, before he was forced to divulge any more encrypting information, the door burst open, and a clicking sound caused Ellie to freeze where she sat, unblinking and completely motionless.

Alexander leapt to his feet, still topless, his wound still stinging, staring wildly about the place looking for whoever had flung the door open.

There appeared to be nobody there, until a faint silhouette of a tall, muscular man fizzled into visibility. Many moments later, the silhouette had developed into the figure of a man that Alexander recognised.

It was Azriel.

'My dear son, what has happened to you?' Azriel did not move, merely scanned Alexander's body, observing his injuries, observing the hopeless desperation in his emerald eyes.

'I fear, this was too great a task for me.' With Azriel's arrival, the immense pressure of emotions that Alexander had been suppressing exploded in his mind and whirred like a Catherine wheel.

Bursting into a hysterical fit of rage, hurt and disappointment in himself, he fell to his knees at his father's feet and sobbed like an infant.

Speechless, having never witnessed anything but vibrance, joy and hopefulness radiating from his son's very being, Azriel could all but watch as his soul shattered to pieces before his eyes.

'You were right.' Alexander spat out between agonised cries and gasping breathlessness. 'I am ordinary. I'm not a true Omniscient.'

Azriel crouched to the floor to face Alexander, and gently gripped his wrists to pull him to his feet.

'This world has changed since your mother, Sebastian and I were selected to intervene with its inhabitants.' Azriel said softly, with certainty. 'The perils we faced whilst here are incomparable to those you have faced during the last few days of your visit.'

'I've failed.' Alexander spluttered. 'Unlike the Omniscients before me, I have failed to achieve the outcome I was sent here to procure.'

Azriel exhaled heavily.

'You forget Concordia.'

Alexander's glazed eyes shot into focus, piercing his father with a yearning glare.

Both men took a seat, ignoring the slightly unsettling frozen woman sat beside them.

'Concordia. Omniscient of Empathy.'

'What happened to her?' Alexander asked, his eyes still fixed on his father.

'We don't know, exactly.' Azriel began, staring at his hands, clasped together and resting on the table. 'She was the last Omniscient to be called to Earth, during a time of war and strife. Unspeakable atrocities were committed by humanity during this time, and Concordia never returned.'

'Never?' Alexander exclaimed.

'Never.' Azriel confirmed, sombrely, neglecting to mention that they had recently discovered she was in fact dead. 'Since her disappearance, I have had visions of her, sick and wounded, abused by humankind, just as you have been. You are not weak, Alexander. You have not failed.'

'Where do I go from here? Alexander asked. 'News of my presence here is all over the world. They know about a mystery planet that is perhaps capable of sustaining human life. I have failed to divert their mission; I've probably fast-tracked their trip to Calathea. They're probably preparing it as we speak.'

'Who is this?' Azriel gestured to Ellie, ignoring Alexander's question.

'This is my friend. She works for NASA and she knows everything about the mission. She also knows that I know about their mission.' Alexander explained, staring at the floor, disappointed in himself.

Azriel was silent for several, thoughtful minutes.

'I want you to persuade your friend to allow you access to her place of work.' He finally instructed. 'From there, you will monitor their progress as closely as you can and do what is required to impede their mission.'

'How do I do that?' Alexander asked, stunned by what his father was instructing him to do.

'You *are* an Omniscient, Alexander. Your intelligence far outshines that of humanity, and you can convince them that Calathea is not a suitable environment, no technology, no heavy machinery. There, they must rely on their own strength and skill, and the ability to live and let live. Here, they may flout their responsibilities to their neighbours and fellow inhabitants of the Earth and lead an entirely selfish life. This philosophy is simply not tolerated in our home.'

'How can I convince them that a place of harmony, serenity and purpose is unsuitable for them when this planet will soon cease to exist?'

'Because this is what you know, this is what you believe. From the depths of your heart, you will find a way to rise from your fall and do what is right.' Azriel declared triumphantly.

'Is it right?' Alexander asked. 'We are essentially orchestrating a massacre. Destruction not just of mankind but all those that have suffered at their hands who must now fall victim to their crimes again. Except this time there is no release.'

'This is the release. They will never have to suffer again.'

'I don't believe that this is the right thing to do. In evil, there is good. There is good in humanity.' Alexander insisted.

Azriel took Alexander's arm and pointed to his bruises.

'Look what they have done to you! They have injured and tormented you, and yet, you still choose to defend them?' Azriel shook his head in disbelief.

'The group of people that subjected me to this violence is a mere atom of the population of this Earth. Among the advocates for violence and affray, there are those that repel such acts of utter folly. Should they not be considered?'

'Alexander, with or without our interference, the outcome will be the same, whether now or in a million years. We are not orchestrating a massacre; we are merely altering the inevitability from sometime in the future to now.' Azriel explained sternly. 'As Omniscients, it goes expressly against our philosophies to deliberately inflict pain and chaos to any other being, which is why the only solution to the crisis of humanity, is this.'

'What if this is not the only solution? What if we were to share our philosophies and teach the inhabitants of this planet to live harmoniously, so that when the fateful day comes, we have achieved the original Omniscient objective? To restore peace to Earth, should it be disturbed.' The ardent young man argued.

'That's just it, Alexander. My entire existence has been devoted to guiding every species to acceptance and peace. Humanity have proven themselves incapable of abiding to such virtues.' Azriel explained again. '*This is the only solution.*'

Alexander offered no further objections. Deep down, he knew his father was right, the outcome was inevitable someday, with or without his intervention.

Despite this realisation, he could not help feeling guilty for the innocent souls that would fall victim to the plan.

The irony was palpable to him, the Omniscients chastise humanity for declaring themselves superior to the species with whom they share their Earth, but seemed to be doing exactly that, by declaring themselves the masters of its fate.

Azriel observed the cogs turning in his son's brain.

'Have we reached an accord?' He directed, as much as asked.

'We have reached an accord.' Alexander replied blankly.

'Very well.' Azriel sighed with relief. 'I shall return to your mother and assure her of your safety. Meanwhile, you will set about your task again. This time, using your knowledge as your weapon.'

They shared an emotional embrace before Azriel's body began to flicker, and faded until he was no longer visible. A strong breeze blew the door shut, and Alexander's outstretched arms were left empty. With that, Ellie was revived from her motionless state, unaware that any time had passed since she asked Alex what he knew about Calathea.

'Well?' She said.

'Perhaps it would be more useful for me to accompany you to your office?' Alexander suggested, much to Ellie's surprise. 'I could covertly assist you with your research.'

'That would be wonderful!' Ellie beamed in utter disbelief. 'How about Monday?'

'Not today?' He asked, fearing that his resolve may have worn off by then.

'I'm not working today, besides we're going to the town hall to listen to the holocaust survivor talk. Do you… still wanna join us?' She asked dubiously.

'Ok.' Alexander smiled half-heartedly.

A little while later, once Alexander's wound was throbbing slightly less, he and Ellie began to walk slowly through the woods toward the city.

They were silent for a time, an air of awkwardness lingering in light of their brief display of romance followed by total disaster and exposure of Alexander's unusual talents and features.

'Alex, I want to make a confession.' Ellie declared quickly, as if trying to spit her words out before she changed her mind.

Alexander turned to look at her and raised his eyebrows kindly, encouraging her to continue.

'I want to explain why I flipped at you in the hospital.' She closed her eyes and exhaled deeply through her nose. 'I've spent my whole life being just, totally dispensable to everyone I've ever known. Friends, family, partners. Nobody has ever been interested in anything about me besides what they can gain from their association with me. As a kid, I didn't have any friends, and my parents put me up for adoption when I was 4. I was in and out of foster homes ever since and I've always been the last thought, bottom of the pile. A nameless, faceless entity in the background.' Her voice began to shake as she stifled tears. 'So, when I met you, and all you seemed to care about was my feelings, I felt like you didn't care what was on the surface, you saw beneath the exterior I present to the world every day. I've never had that, it was strange, but I felt like I was starting to trust you . So, then to discover that there was this whole other person in there, this whole agenda that you had been hiding from me, it touched a nerve because I revered you as this… this sincere, sweet guy that I… It was the first time I'd let anyone see anything but the bitch I've learned to be, because for the first time I felt like someone cared, and I didn't have to hide anymore. But I'm just a pawn in your "public service". Useful to know.'

Tears streamed down her face, and her cheeks flushed as she realised she'd completely veered onto a tangent, revealing more of herself than she ever had to another person, perhaps even more than she had ever revealed to herself, without removing a single item of clothing.

There was a long silence before Alexander responded, visibly hurt, surprised by the fragility of his friend, despite her strong exterior. Browning leaves crunched beneath their feet as they strolled in the direction of the city. Ellie wiped her tears, discouraged by Alexander's silence, fearing that she had driven him away by reaching out for support, accustomed to being abandoned in her times of need ever since she was a child.

'You are useful to know.' He finally said. Ellie turned her head sharply; her blood shot eyes meeting Alexander's. 'From the very moment I met you, I've felt at home. There is something very different about you and your attitude toward, well, everything. You challenged everything I have been taught to believe about humanity. You made me question why I came here in the first place. If I was doing the right thing.'

Ellie's expression softened.

'What exactly have you been taught to believe about humanity?'

Alexander let out a long sigh.

'That they are a species beyond help. A species that have been given countless opportunities to mend the error of their ways and dismissed them without a tear. A species without scruples or decency for their neighbours or fellow inhabitants of a planet they have utterly abused.' He rambled without drawing breath. 'Since I've been here, I've witnessed things that both fully support and contradict these allegations. There are people desperately trying to care for those that have been mistreated by their less enlightened neighbours, but the only ones that seem to really make a difference or have any kind of influence… are the less enlightened ones.'

'Crazed by power and willing to seek it out whatever the cost, paid only by others.'

'Exactly that. Truthfully, I don't know what I would have done here, had I not met you.' Alexander admitted. 'Of course, I wouldn't have been stabbed and treated quite so barbarously…'

They both laughed.

'But you've definitely put things into perspective.'

'I'm getting the feeling that whatever you're here to do, has something to do with the almost paranormal changes to the Earth's course in its orbit?' Ellie's intonation rose with her suspicion.

There was another long silence.

'Alex-'

'-Yes.' He interrupted.

'Can you tell me what?' Ellie rose her right eyebrow softly, tilting her head to the left slightly, urging him to oblige her with an explanation.

'How long do you have?' Alexander replied in an attempt to divert her.

'How long do you need?' Ellie said deeply, in a sarcastically playful manner.

Alexander didn't reply. He looked at her with a timid and uncertain expression, and her smirk dissolved into a neutral countenance.

'You're not gonna give this up easy, are ya, Alex?' She sighed.

'It's not that I don't trust you to understand, I do.' He nodded. 'I've lost faith in the whole thing, to be honest.'

Ellie shoved her hands in her pockets as she admitted defeat. Discovering his necklace with her left hand, she opened her mouth to let Alexander know that she had kept it for him, she noticed Chelsea up ahead.

'Alex.' Chelsea stepped forward and gently held both of his hands, looking around to see if anyone recognised him. 'I'm not sure it's such a good idea for you to be out in public. There's a lot of people looking for you. Did they take any pictures of you in the hospital?'

'They did.' He answered the police officer. 'I don't think they'll be able to recover them, though.'

His face was filled with shame as he recalled his aggressive behaviour.

'Ok, well, the police are speaking to the doctors in the hospital that treated you. They've hired a professional artist to sketch an impression of your face so the public know to keep an eye out of you. I guess it'll take a day or two to complete but after that, you might wanna keep a low profile.' She said quietly.

Chelsea had given him a lot to think about, but what he heard next gave him even more.

They entered the dimly lit building with a raised stage and an arc of chairs surrounding it. Once they had settled, an elderly lady with olive, wrinkled skin and dark, short, wispy hair entered the stage.

Her name was Gerda Weissmann Klein.

Chapter 10 – Gerda Weissmann Klein & a Rare Spirit

'The murder of my mother saved my life.

Mama and I held hands tightly, as we marched along in pairs. We heard cries and screams ahead of us. A cane hit our hands. The cane pointed at me, a voice shouted, "How old?".

18.

The cane shoved me aside. I knew mama was marching in the opposite direction. I was herded toward a group where my friends stood.

I did not see mama.

I just remember a tremendous panic, and shortly thereafter, some trucks arrived.

We were loaded on the truck and I was taken away from my mother, so I jumped off. A very slight, small man picked me up and he threw me onto the truck and he says: "You are too young to die".

I glared at him.

I hate you! I screamed. I hate you!

Then, above all the screams coming from behind the barbed wire, I heard my mother.

Mama! Mama! I called.

Above all the confused, painful cries, I heard mama's voice again.

"Be strong."

And I heard it again like an echo.

"Be strong."

Those were my mother's last words to me.

My family gone, my childhood gone.

I was in the hand of a brutal enemy.

Those whom the SS judged unable to work were killed. Those who could work would be used for forced labour, under punishing conditions.

I had a friend by the name of Ilse Kleinzahler.

I'd known Ilse since childhood. Ilse was a little younger than I, her mother and my mother were close friends. My mother always told me what a well-behaved, nice, good-looking girl Ilse was, how beautifully she played the piano, how I should be more like her, and predictably, I hated to play with her.

Together, we were sold into the same camp. The SS men guarded the entrance, and counted us as we entered. Once inside, what we saw was sickening.

Several living skeletons stretched out begging hands. We were bitter cold and hungry and everything, and we didn't get anything to eat for days, literally.

One morning, on the way to the factory in which we worked, she found a single raspberry in the gutter. She carried that treasure in her pocket all day long, to present it to me on a leaf, which she plucked through the barbed wire.

One, slightly bruised, dust-covered raspberry becomes your entire possession, and you give this treasure to a friend.

In the camps we became to each other, the only family we had.

{1945}

Our orders were to be shipped to a murder camp, and we started a march known as a Death March. And I was coughing terribly, I had a very bad cold. And in the morning, very early, the doors opened to an incredible picture. There was freshly fallen snow for as far as the eye could see.

Way, way ahead, 4000 girls, and on the side was SS men and women, and they lifted their whips and they said "Forward, march".

And we held hands and we took the first step. We all knew that this was going to be the first step to the end of the road, either to liberation or to, to doom.

We marched for over three months, covering more than 350 miles on foot. And of the enormous number, fewer than 120 survived.

Ilse wasn't well at all, and one of the most shocking things was that one of our other friends had somehow found two potatoes. I gave Ilse the potato and she said she wasn't hungry.

That was the most incredible statement, not to be hungry.

And she said to me "You eat it."

She said something incredible. She said "I'm not angry at anyone, I hope no one is angry at me." She said to me "You have to promise me, that you're going to go on for one more week."

A week was a very long time.

And she said, "Promise."

I said, "I'll try."

And I held her, and we both fell asleep.

I woke up, but she didn't.

Ilse died in my arms, on a wet meadow in Czechoslovakia. She had just turned 18.

She never tasted another raspberry again.

There were American planes overhead, the shooting of the American artillery close by, and of course, the SS wanted to finish the witnesses to their deeds.

Our small number of 120 were locked into an abandoned bicycle factory, onto which a time bomb was attached. And they barricaded the doors with chains and things, and they told us that we are going to be killed. And I said to myself, well, I'm going to start thinking what it would be like on a night like this at home, being in the garden with my parents.

So, if they kill me, that's the memory I want.

We waited and waited and waited.

Suddenly it started to rain. A torrential, magical rain.

The bomb and the timer did not connect.

At dawn, we heard voices as the doors were thrust open. I saw a strange-looking car, coming down a gentle hill.

On the hood of the car, not the despised swastika, but the white star of the American army.

There were two men in that car. One jumped out, and I knew what I had to say. And I said to him "We are Jewish, you know."

For a very long time, at least to me it seemed very long, he didn't answer me. And then his own voice betrayed his emotion. He was wearing dark glasses, I couldn't see his eyes.

He said, "So am I."

I told him that most of the girls were inside, but were too ill to walk. He asked me to come with him.

At first, I didn't understand it. And when I understood it, I could not believe it.

He simply held the door open for me and let me precede him. And in this great gesture, he restored me to humanity.

I weighed 68 pounds, my hair was white, I was in rags, I had not had a bath in three years. And here was this very handsome young American, holding the door open for me.

I remember that aura of him, of the awe, of the disbelief in daylight, to really see someone who fought for our freedom. He looked like, like God to me.

"The most unforgettable and remarkable thing that happened then was that this young woman who had shown me inside and made a sweeping gesture over this whole scene, and said the following words: Noble be man, merciful and good. And it was hard for me to believe that she, in that condition, under those circumstances, had been able to summon a line from a poem by the German poet Goethe. A poem called "The Divine". By doing so, she chose to underscore the grim irony of what I was seeing there more effectively than anything else that she might have said."

And this first young American for Liberation Day is now my husband.

He not only opened the door for me, but the door to my life and my future.

I brought our youngest child, our son, home from the hospital. I held him in my arms, and realised that Ilse never had that privilege. She lies in an unmarked grave, somewhere in Czechoslovakia.

The week that she compelled me to go on was May 7th.

A week later, exactly to the day, perhaps to the very hour of her death, we were liberated by American forces.

Over the years, of course, she is often in my thoughts. On the day I was invited to a bridal shower, I looked at the excitement of the young bridesmaids, the radiance in the face of the young bride. I looked at her through different eyes. You see, she is my daughter. And she is named for my friend, Ilse.

I saw so much nobility of spirit in the camps.

To know that the legacy of the camps is not the legacy of the horror, but of the greatness of people.

The very humanity which existed there in the face of such incredible inhumanity.

When you help someone else with your friendship and your caring, there is a part of immortality. Because you live in someone else's life, and in other people's hopes.

And this is really what it's all about, to invest yourself in others.

Like my little friend Ilse.'

Chapter 11 – An Altering Perspective

Alexander was simply stunned by Gerda's story. She struck a chill in his very heart.

He could not conceive how any person could bring themselves to treat another being the way millions of innocent people were treated during the war Concordia had perished in the face of.

More unbelievable, was the total devotion to one another that the brave men and women displayed to one another, at a time of desperate need.

'I'm not angry at anyone. I hope no one is angry at me.'

Ilse's words and Gerda's voice circulated Alexander's mind, and he was brought to a spellbinding realisation.

Ilse, a remarkably unselfish young woman with a phenomenally pure spirit, urged her friend to continue to fight for her life and her freedom…

She was Concordia's spirit.

Subjected to misery and brutality, the trueness, tenaciousness, and nobility of their souls shone through the darkness of the clouds raining over their heads, cast by the barbaric beliefs of the monstrous Nazis, dispelled by those that fought for their freedom.

Concordia's spirit was broken by the mistreatment of Ilse's purity, yet she knew that liberation was but a week away, and willed her friend to survive for the freedom each and every person subjected to the devastating effects of the Holocaust deserved.

Alexander wished he could rally every Gerda, every Ilse and every innocent creature and whisk them to Calathea to live a life unthreatened by the callous intentions of the people left to perish with the Earth.

Bolstered with resolve to complete his task, on Monday Ellie and Alexander entered the space centre together.

That very same day, Chelsea also went to work. On her desk, was the sketch of Alexander's face. Identical to him.

It was her job to file a report on the wanted man she was assumed to have no connection to.

'You sure you wanna do this?' Ellie asked with a supportive squeeze of his fingers.

'No!' He declared, taking her hand and holding it firmly. 'Let's do it.'

Ellie and Alexander approached the entrance to the space centre, hand in hand.

The security guard that had dismissed him weeks ago didn't seem to recognise Alexander as they drew nearer, more interested in another detail…

He wolf whistled.

'New boyfriend, Johnson?' He teased as he turned to open the door for them.

Ellie threw Alexander's hand from hers.

'Fuck off, door man.' She scowled, shoving past him, Alexander in tow.

Wires, computer screens, beeping, flashing monitors filled his wide eyes as he stared around the interior of the impressive building like a bull calf that had strayed from his stall. Unimpressed by these familiar sights, Ellie strode on purposefully, occasionally turning back to check Alexander had not wandered in the wrong direction.

The ceiling towered above them as they approached a large set of glass doors decorated with a silver plaque that read:

'Eleanor Johnson

Head of Earth Observatory'

Ellie threw open the doors and retrieved a 'visitor' lanyard from her desk. She threw it to Alexander.

'Put this on.' She instructed.

Ellie sat at her desk behind three monitors that flashed to life with the touch of a button. Alexander's eyes lit up as the systems launched and all manner of numbers, messages and outstanding tasks pinged onto the screens, his pupils darting around as he attempted to read everything that flickered into view and disappeared in a matter of milliseconds.

Once the novelty of the technology that was simply alien to him had worn off, he scanned Ellie while she worked. She sat with her right leg draped across her knee, black opaque tights hugged her legs and a tight, black midi dress clung to her slender figure, revealing a tease of her cleavage. Her hair was scraped into a bun as it often was, but much neater than usual, with two wisps of hair framing her face, square glasses adding to her professional and attractive appearance.

After several minutes of typing in silence, Ellie spun in her chair and caught the one next to it with her foot, wheeling it toward Alexander. She nodded her head, gesturing for him to take a seat.

Before introducing him to any of her colleagues, William Hickory in particular, Ellie briefed Alexander with regards to what to expect from each of them. She explained that Jonny Samson, junior observer, a

5"11 dark skinned, handsome and muscular young man would be most accommodating toward him, while his team are less personable, but still pleasant. Mr Hickory, on the other hand…

'Remember that asshole I was telling you about when we first met?' She began. 'That's my boss, and he's guaranteed to be uncongenial and rude. You should also be aware that preparations for sending a rocket to our mystery planet are underway and it is likely to happen within the next two weeks. Production of the space shuttle we began engineering when we first discovered the planet is also due to be completed within a month.'

Alexander bit the inside of his cheek in an attempt to conceal the growing discontent within him as a result of the news Ellie had just delivered to him. His family, his home, his dear sweet Wilbur were now at risk of exposure, a risk he could only attribute to his own exposure on Earth.

'Any questions?' Ellie asked, noticing his somewhat dazed expression.

'I don't think so.' He lied, wondering what sending a rocket to Calathea meant for his home and his loved ones there.

'Great, let's go!' Ellie tapped the table with her two hands and rose to her feet.

Holding the door open for Alexander, she told him to follow the corridor and enter the first door to his left. The corridor was dark with floor and ceiling lights to make it navigable, revealing the satellite images of space dotted across the black walls, as well as images of rockets and Neil Armstrong.

He reached the door Ellie had described, and waited for her to catch up. She ushered him into the room filled with monitors just like the ones on her desk, and huge screens projecting confusing graphs and images that Alexander couldn't comprehend. There were around 20 people tapping keyboards, discussing the enlarged images on the screens and generally milling around.

'Johnson!' Jonny Samson beamed, noticing her from across the room. 'What're you doing in here with the little people?' He joked, tapping her shoulder.

'Very funny, I'm here to introduce Alex here.' She said, putting her hands on his shoulders. 'He's here to observe our progress and provide support wherever he can with our mystery planet.'

It struck Alexander just how good she was at concealing her emotions and presenting a bold face when barely a day ago she was pouring her bleeding heart out to him.

'Nice to meet you, Alex!' Jonny said sincerely, shaking Alexander's hand.

'Nice to meet you, sir.' Alexander replied.

'This way, please.' Jonny held his arm out to the left and led Alexander to his desk, strewn with papers which he collected and placed neatly under Alexander's nose.

'As the various data sheets, reports and graphs I have just given you will testify, Nasa along with our partners are currently developing, testing and maturing critical components of propulsion technologies that will enable us to safely transfer human beings from Earth to this planet.' He began, circling structures on his computer screen with the lid of the pen in his hand. 'Before we can think about sending people there, however, we will need to launch a rocket into space in the direction of our mystery planet to gauge the distance etcetera so that we can accurately calculate the propulsion and thrust required to successfully complete the trip. We'll also attach a camera and various components that will display the terrain, atmospheric conditions, and other details that we need to decipher to prepare for the trip. You with me so far?'

'Yes, I think so.'

'Using satellite images, we have identified large bodies of water to be present on this planet which suggest that the atmospheric conditions may be, or soon be sufficient to sustain human life.' Jonny continued enthusiastically.

'This is deemed even more probable since some kind of "super human" has been identified right here in the States! If we are correct in our surmise and he is actually from our mystery planet, we could be looking at making the first trip in weeks, if he is capable of surviving in Earth's atmospheric conditions, it's likely they are the same.'

'Why is it so important that you send people to this planet?' Alexander asked.

'It's imperative that we enable human life on another planet because the Earth's course in the solar system has diverted toward the sun at an alarming rate, which will result in it being engulfed much, much sooner than we had expected. In order to sustain human life, we must find another planet suitable for us to live on.'

'Will it be possible to take every person from Earth to Ca- ...the mystery planet?' Alexander's heart thudded as he almost slipped up.

'Unfortunately, that will not be possible.' Samson stated matter-of-factly.

'How will you select who deserves to continue the human race?' Alexander challenged, cynically.

'Uh, well I don't think that will be up to me.' Samson replied, looking uncomfortable.

'Will you just be taking humans, or will any other species be included in the relocation?'

Jonny shook his head.

'So far, we have opted not to include any other species.'

Alexander was disappointed, yet unsurprised.

'So, the selected elites will be living on a planet with no wildlife?'

At that moment, William Hickory entered the Observatory Quarters with Ellie Johnson.

'Who's the tree hugger, Johnson?' Hickory grunted, scowling at Alexander.

'Mr Hickory, this is Alexander, he will be observing and supporting our progress with our mystery planet.' Ellie explained, raising her right eyebrow at the 'tree hugger' sat before her, looking slightly offended.

'It doesn't sound like he's helping so far, Eleanor.' Said Hickory, staring at her sternly.

'I happen to agree with him.' Ellie declared, returning his harsh glare. 'Who in this world has the right to decide who gets to start a new life on another planet, and who goes up in smoke with the planet we have all called home since the beginning of time?'

'The people that have the means to make it happen, Johnson.' Hickory answered back in a raised voice. 'If you fraternised less with the lower orders, perhaps you'd understand that.'

There was silence across the entire room, and a sea of stunned faces turned to look at William Hickory, a tall, fat man with a shiny patch of scalp in the centre of his short, grey hair.

'I find your attitude unfathomable, Mr Hickory.' Alexander said coolly, standing opposite him.

William totally disregarded Alexander's existence, turning away from him and exiting the room.

'Johnson, I want the first stage of the rocket launch prepared and on my desk by the end of today, and your tree-hugging friend off this premises.' His voice trailed off with every step he took.

'Congratulations, that's the longest anyone has ever gone before pissing that asshole off!' Ellie remarked, gathering the paperwork from Samson's desk. 'Jonny, I'll look over your proposal in my office and get back to you with any alterations as soon as I can. Keep this one on a leash, in the meantime.' She winked and slapped Jonny's arm as she turned and retreated to her office.

'Honestly, Alex, I agree with most of your opinions, but you won't get far broadcasting them around here.' Samson advised him, turning to face his laptop.

That evening, Ellie returned from work to find Chelsea sat with her chin resting on her palms as she stared down at a newspaper. Pictured in the centre of the front page, was a sketch. A sketch that looked nothing like Alexander.

Meanwhile, he sat alone in his lodge and thought hard about the discoveries he had made during the day. It was obvious that those in a position to decide who was eligible to escape their inevitable fate, were not capable of making a decision that would benefit any but themselves. Despite his Omniscient abilities, his trusting nature renders him unable to bewitch the minds of others, having only interacted with Calathean beings, he was unfamiliar with such selfishness.

He spent the next couple of weeks quietly observing Jonny and Ellie preparing for the launch of the first rocket to Calathea. It took all his strength not to divulge his true identity and plead with them not to invade his home and endanger those closest to him.

With the day of the launch nigh upon them, Alexander stalled for time and tried to throw as may spanners into the works as possible. His desperate actions stooped to hiding critical papers associated with the mission, but alas his pitiful efforts came to no avail.

The fateful day arrived, the sky an angry grey. Rain slicing through the air, thunder roaring, lighting striking.

A crowd of Ellie's team surrounded the large screens in the observatory quarter of the building, Ellie and Jonny at the front, accompanied by an anxious Alexander.

'Why do you look so nervous, my ass is on the line here not yours!' Ellie remarked as she noticed Alexanders sheet-white complexion.

If only she knew, he thought. Much more was at stake for Alexander. His time at the space centre taught him that many missions end in failure, and the only consequence is a harsh word from a tall, fat man who thought very highly of himself.

Alexander, however, had a responsibility to alter the very existence of humanity, assigned by a being with the power to vanquish an entire planet and all that exists within it.

The screen displayed the tall, slim rocket equipped with cameras and all kinds of devices beyond Alexander's understanding.

'Mystery rocket ready to launch in 10, 9, 8, 7, 6, 5, 4, 3, 2, 1!' Ellie counted into a walkie talkie, her colleagues joining in the count down.

An enormous explosion beneath the rocket propelled it into space with a cloud of exhaust smoke.

An excruciating silence filled the room as the rocket ripped through the clouds at an exorbitant speed with no indication of descending. The mysterious missile with the power to expose the divine interventions at work reached the stratosphere, disappeared from the view of the ground cameras and shot into satellite images also displayed on screen.

Ellie inhaled sharply.

Alexander's knuckles were white from gripping the back of the chair for dear life.

The rocket kept climbing.

Ellie's eyes widened with hopeful speculation.

The rocket reached the mesosphere and began to lose momentum. Just before it reached the edge of the mesosphere and entered the thermosphere, the rocket plummeted back toward the crust of the Earth, and Alexander let out a sigh of relief that his peers regarded as disappointment, thankfully.

'It happens, Alex. None of our missions succeed first time around.' Ellie consoled him, rubbing his back. 'Good news is the rocket was so close to exiting the Earth's atmosphere, it'll only take a few minor adjustments and we can try again this week!'

Ellie's optimism unsettled Alexander and the sound of his father instructing him to use his knowledge as a deterrent for humanity to invade their home rang in his ears. He had not yet divulged the fact that he was the 'Alien in America'.

Perhaps he should.

Days later, they were ready to reattempt their mission to expose Calathea for all it was.

This time, it was a success.

The rocket soared through the atmosphere until it exited the Earth entirely, heading right for the direction of Alexander's blissful sanctuary.

Ellie squeezed his hand as she watched the rocket hurtle toward her mystery planet with glee. The symbol of Alexander's failure contaminated Calathea, a place that had been protected from the mercilessness of humanity for so long, now at risk of being overthrown by this frighteningly tenacious species.

On Calathea, the lazy waterfall flowing tranquilly inside Althea and Azriel's cavern caught fire with furious flames as the foreign, unwelcome object entered the land of new beginnings, intended to remain unencumbered by the interference of humanity.

The rocket came crashing to the ground and plummeted into the sand as Azriel, Althea and Sebastian watched.

At the space centre, thrilled colleagues hugged and cheered and clapped as Ellie confirmed the rocket had landed on their mystery planet.

Ellie squealed words of excitement in Alexander's face, expecting him to return her felicitations, but he couldn't hear her.

Images of horrifying scenarios blinded and deafened him, arousing tremendous suspicion among the elated employees, dizzy with excitement.

'Engage the camera device so we can have a look around.' Ellie directed as her colleague executed her orders with a series of clicks and taps on his computer.

The flickering image focussed to reveal the divine scenery, turquoise ocean shining beneath the sunlight, white sand dotted with vibrantly coloured shells, and three Omniscients staring at the camera that rose on a metal rod from the body of the rocket. The curious and adorable Wilbur approached with caution and sniffed the object.

A wave of despair washed over Alexander's soul as everything he ever cared about became the distinct object of human desire.

Realising they were in grave danger, Sebastian grabbed a handful of sand and threw it across the air toward the unfamiliar structure, forming a black blanket as it travelled that pulled the daylight from the sky and filled it instead with an impenetrable darkness.

Chapter 12 – Loose Lips

Alexander's heart was beating like a drum against his rib cage, and he could feel the blood pulsating through his veins and his vision was blurred. His ears rang with the sound of ignorant people questioning the identity of his family.

'This is fantastic!' Ellie gasped. 'Jonny, you were right all along!'

Alexander failed to conceal his worry any longer.

'Alex, what the hell is your problem?' She snorted, spotting his flushed cheeks and feverish expression. 'This is great news! It looks like we could actually live there, we could send the first astronaut there soon!'

He said nothing.

Ignoring him, Ellie peered over Jonny's shoulder, who now sat at his desk and analysed the data screening from Calathea, calculating the atmospheric pressure, concentration of gases in the air and comparing them to those of Earth.

'Looks like the level of Oxygen in the air is higher than here, with a lot less background radiation. The Nitrogen is similar, carbon dioxide considerably lower.' Jonny reported.

'Could be safer to live there than here!' Ellie laughed. 'What about the creatures, can we get a better look at them?'

Alexander's stomach churned sickeningly.

'Whoever they are, they better get ready for some visitors!' Jonny announced, cheerfully.

He began enlarging the images of Althea, Azriel and Sebastian, disregarding Wilbur. Ellie watched over his shoulder. Projected on the screens, the images were pixelated and unclear, but with several clicks of Jonny's mouse, their faces were clarified and recognisable.

'Alex, you look kinda like one of the guys on that planet...' Ellie said slowly, zooming in on Azriel's face. 'Your jaw and your eyes, they're...'

A loud silence filled the room as everybody turned to look at Alexander, and seemingly reached the same conclusion.

'What's that under your shirt?' Jonny Samson asked, pointing at the faintly visible bandage across his stab wound. 'Wasn't that alien guy stabbed right there in his chest?'

Whispers of disbelief circulated the room as Ellie's colleagues began to realise that the mysterious man they had been speculating, had been in their very presence for weeks.

'If that guy's his dad, does that mean the woman is his sister?' Jordan Williams piped up from across the room. 'The things I would do to her!'

Alexander heard the grubby young man boast.

A flush of burning anger rose from his feet and detonated in his head, but on the exterior he was neutral.

'I will not let you destroy my home.' Alexander said softly, the bewildered people around him staring at him like he was crazy. 'And you will never lay a finger on my mother.'

He towered over the young man that had sexualised the very woman that gave Alexander's life, despite him being much taller and much more muscular, he didn't seem to intimidate him.

'I would *love..* to *fuck* your mother.' The insolent man declared, leaning in to Alexander's face arrogantly.

Alexander took a shaky inward breath, desperately trying to control his mind and quell his anger.

'You can watch if you want.'

He turned away, smirking, and Alexander could not contain himself. His rage engulfed all sense and restraint, and in a moment of madness, he raised his right arm and belted the man around the head with such force that he flew across the room, taking several computers out with him. The force he had swung his arm with ripped his shirt, exposing his bound chest, specs of blood beginning to seep through the bandage.

His human kryptonite shattered all the virtues he embodied, eclipsed by his hatred of some of their unfathomable habits, he allowed his anger to direct his behaviour.

The commotion he created summoned the security guards along with William Hickory.

'God, it's that tree hugger, get him out!' Hickory ordered, angrily examining the damage he had caused.

Before the security guards had seized Alexander to forcibly remove him from the premises, Hickory noticed the bandage around his chest, catching sight of the 'Aliens in America?' article that had landed on the floor near where he was stood.

Alexander began to tear the sheets detailing the progress of the mystery planet mission, throwing the fractions of paper to the floor.

'I will not let you take this any further. You had your opportunity for redemption, and you wasted it in favour of-'

The security guard interrupted him with a large dose of sedative that drained his consciousness instantly.

'We've got you now.' Hickory swaggered, standing over Alexander.

This time, when he woke, the measures restraining him were much more vigorous.

He was encased in a large glass dome. Reinforced glass.

'If only we had some kind of drug we could give him that would make him tell us who the hell he is.' Hickory daydreamed, arms folded, looking thoughtful.

'This isn't Harry Potter, Dickory.' Ellie remarked sarcastically. 'We've gotta be clever about this because he could be a huge help to us. But also a huge hinderance.'

'I think you ought to be clever, Johnson. Consider the appropriate way to talk to a man with the power to destroy your career.'

'Who would lead this mission if you fired me? You?' She sniggered, and strutted out of the isolation unit, leaving Alexander alone with William Hickory.

'What are we to do, Azriel?' Althea asked, pacing the candlelit cavern. 'Should we go to help Alexander?'

'No. We trust him to see this through.' Azriel replied sternly.

'We have trusted him from the very beginning. Look where that has got us.' She challenged.

'If we leave, we risk being detained alongside Alexander, and our land being captured by those it was created to avoid.' Azriel explained. 'You once lectured me about patience and allowing our son the time to prove himself. My love, I must ask you to heed your own advice.'

As the candlelight flickered on Althea's discontented face, her son flickered back to life.

He lay on his back for a moment, taking several deep breaths, staring at the ceiling above him. When he eventually rose to sit, the first thing he saw, was William Hickory, accompanied by Christian Evernaut.

The panes of glass separating them muffled the conversation between the two men observing Alexander like an animal in a zoo. After a few minutes, Hickory exited the room, closing the door firmly behind him. Christian took a seat and watched Alexander closely, his right leg crossed over his left, a notepad resting on his thigh and pen a in his hand.

The psychologist did not speak, nor did he take his watchful eye off of Alexander, recording his every move in his notepad.

Realising what was happening, Alexander made no attempt to flee his cage, but sat on his bed and stared forward blankly, wondering how in the world he was going to escape this time.

Meanwhile, Ellie was forced to attend a disciplinary meeting to discuss why she kept Alexander's true identity a secret, truthfully explaining that she was not certain that he had come from a different planet, just that he was suspiciously well-informed about their mission.

Having successfully convinced HR that one does not usually consider the possibility that a new acquaintance was not born on the only planet previously known to sustain human life, Ellie paid Alexander a visit.

Dismissing Dr Evernaut, Ellie spoke to the caged man through a microphone projecting through a speaker into the glass box.

'You have a lot of explaining to do.' She said sternly. 'And I'm gonna have a lot of trouble getting you out of here if you don't cooperate.'

Feeling defeated, Alexander decided it was time to trust Ellie, as she had trusted him.

'Very well, I will explain everything to you.' He replied, pressing his thumbs into his index fingers through closed fists in an attempt to fight his nerves. 'Can you come in here so we can talk in private?'

Ellie was hesitant.

'You better not try anything, Alex.'

He held up his hands and backed away from the glass to allow Ellie to enter. She released the button that powered the microphone and her fingers brushed the one beside it as the turned to approach the entrance to the box, switching on a small, circular red light on the panel.

They sat beside one another on the bed, and Alexander decided to take a risk.

'There is no delicate way to explain this, but I was not born on Earth. I was born on your "mystery planet", my home is Calathea.'

'Calathea?'

'It's a symbol of new beginnings, much like the planet.' He continued. 'Unfortunately, beginnings usually go hand in hand with… ends.'

'Oh, God… Does this have something to do with the Earth hurtling toward the sun?' Ellie's bewildered expression suddenly changed to one of abject terror.

Alexander nodded.

'I belong to a family of Omniscient spirits. They have existed since the beginning of time and observed Earth and all its inhabitants. They were selected by Anad, the Omniscient Commander, to restore peace to the Earth should unrest rear its head.'

Ellie was visibly speechless.

'The last Omniscient spirit to be called to Earth was destroyed during her efforts to end World War II, and Anad decided that humanity was a species that could not be helped, and the only way to solve the "crisis of humanity" was to work with nature and hasten the demise of the planet, along with its inhabitants, and start afresh with on Calathea with a more enlightened species of people.'

'And you're here to stop us from leaving Earth?'

'Yes.' Alexander sighed heavily. 'Yes, I am here to stop humanity from leaving Earth and invading Calathea.'

They sat in silence for a painful few minutes.

'It all makes sense now.' Ellie finally said. 'I mean, none of this makes sense, it's all kinda terrifying to be honest but it definitely explains your behaviour.'

'I only didn't tell you before because I didn't trust myself to find the words.' Alexander explained, rubbing his forehead with his hands. 'In any case, it doesn't matter because I've done the precise opposite of preventing it.'

'Tell me about this "Calathea", what is it like?' She asked.

Alexander smiled and breathed a calming air as he travelled home in his mind.

'It's peaceful, it's beautiful, it's simple. Stunning scenery, wildlife, coastlines. No machinery, no technology, no hate, no destruction… Just existing to be happy. No stressful workplace, living as you want and allowing others to do likewise.'

'Does it not get boring, everything being so perfect and predictable?' Ellie asked again, accustomed to the stress and uncertainty often presented by life on Earth as we know it.

'No, it doesn't at all. Since I've been here, I've experienced emotional turmoil that I've been unencumbered by for my whole life. There's nothing boring about being truly at peace, Ellie.' Alexander replied thoughtfully.

'I think I'd get bored, you need a little excitement, uncertainty, living in the moment because you never know what shit life is gonna throw at you next!' She responded passionately.

'I'd rather wake up knowing that there's a whole beautiful world within my reach, just waiting for me to go and experience it without some dread in my heart that my peace may be snatched from my grasp at any given moment.'

'I guess we're different that way. So, what's the deal with your family? I take it from your outburst that it was your mom and dad on the screen?'

'Yes, my mother, father, and uncle Sebastian. Not to mention my dog, Wilbur.' He continued. 'And I let them down. My father always said I was ordinary, that I didn't have any real Omniscient talent. Looks like he's right.'

'Didn't you say that the Omniscient trying to end the war was killed?'

'Yes, but-'

'You look alive to me!' She stated encouragingly. 'This isn't over, Alex.'

'How can you possibly think that? There's no way I can keep mankind from entering Calathea.'

'What if I help you?' Ellie suggested to a staggered Alexander.

Though he trusted Ellie, he could not help but wonder whether she was offering genuine help or whether she just wanted entrée into the inner circle. At this stage, he had little more to lose and even less to gain by alienating his only comrade on Earth.

'Oh, by the way, Alex I have your-'

Before she could finish her sentence, William Hickory and Christian Evernaut burst through the door and were met by the sight of Ellie and Alexander connecting.

Mr Hickory pressed his index finger to the microphone button:

'I'm guessing you didn't intend to broadcast that entire conversation to my office, Johnson?' He smirked. 'And now, we have all the evidence we need to sign you off this mission and get a space shuttle to Calathea.'

He released his finger from the button and swaggered out of the isolation unit, leaving Alexander and Ellie staring despairingly at one another.

Ellie was indeed struck off and pending investigation, while Alexander realised he had absolutely no hope of stopping Mr Hickory from sending the first space craft to his home.

He was trapped in the glass box, refraining from utilising his Omniscient strength that could allow his release, in favour of at least remaining at the space centre to keep track of their progress, as opposed to being held hostage by doctors examining him so barbarously. He couldn't help but wonder why they were still holding him there, when he had already accidentally filled in the missing pieces of the jigsaw puzzle that paved the way for their invasion of Calathea.

Rather worryingly, Alexander had several visits from NASA employees that he did not recognise, where they measured his body from head to toe and recorded his measurements in meticulous detail. He hadn't seen Ellie for several weeks and he was completely isolated from anybody that he could possibly convince to divulge even the smallest detail about the imminent departure of *Space Shuttle Calathea.*

Ellie had even less luck gathering intel on the mission, all her former colleagues had ceased communication with her, under strict instructions from William Hickory, and she was stripped of her ID card that would allow her entry to the space centre. Unsurprisingly, the security guards were happy to oblige given their hostile relationship with Ellie.

All she could do was read the newspaper articles detailing interviews with William Hickory, defaming her considerably:

CHIEF SCIENTIST WILLIAM HICKORY LEADS MISSION TO SAVE HUMANITY

Earlier this year, William Hickory, NASA Goddard Space Flight Centre's Chief Scientist discovered a planet displaying promising indications of compatibility with human life, just as the Earth's course suspiciously diverted toward the sun posing a serious threat to all life on Earth. This discovery came at a time when a Washington Hospital performed life-saving surgery on who they thought to be a 'local hero', stabbed in the chest while defending a young man from teenage bullies. This 'hero' was identified to be an extra-terrestrial who has been exposed to originate from the mystery planet named 'Calathea'.

Head of Earth Observatory at the space centre, Eleanor Johnson was leading the exhibition, but recently discovered to be in contact with said 'hero', and offered him assistance to sabotage the mission, when she mistakenly streamed the conversation directly to Mr Hickory's office. He released the following statement:

'Johnson was hanging by a thread as it was, her volatile attitude and brazen arrogance already threatened her job security, but her sworn allegiance with the alien wandering our streets was the straw that broke the camel's back. Fortunately, her connection to the young man equipped us with the knowledge we needed to finalise our plans to travel to "Calathea". We plan to launch the space shuttle in a mere few weeks.'

'God, you're such a dick.' Ellie breathed, slamming the newspaper down on her kitchen table.

Dressed in sweats and her hair in a mess, she looked exhausted.

'Another unflattering article?' Chelsea asked, observing her roommate's annoyance.

'Oh yeah...' Ellie slid the article across the table to her.

'Volatile attitude and brazen arrogance? Is this guy for real?' Chelsea cried. 'If that's true then you learned it from that fat bastard!'

'Chelsea, please don't go there or I'm likely to explode.' Ellie stated, flinging her glasses off her nose and burying her head in her hands so hard she slapped her forehead.

'What are you gonna do about Alex? Do you know what's happening to him?' Chelsea changed the subject.

'Honestly, I have no idea. I wouldn't be surprised if they carted him back to the hospital to be locked in a cell and hooked up to machines.'

'Surely, they'll keep him in captivity at the space centre to answer their questions?'

'Yeah, you might be right actually.' Ellie considered. 'It doesn't matter either way, I'm not allowed anywhere near the space centre and if he is at the hospital, they won't let me near him if they know who I am.'

'D'you think he'll try and stop them going to his home one last time?'

'No. There is nothing he can do now.' Ellie snapped. 'If it wasn't for me broadcasting his entire confession to Dickory's office, we might have had a shot at stopping them. But not now. I can't bear to think of him trapped in that glass box, all alone.'

'Maybe we should dress up in sexy black outfits and break him outta there, like in the movies!' Chelsea joked, trying to lighten the dark mood.

'This isn't a joke, Chelsea. I told you why he was trying to sabotage the whole mission in the first place, and if it weren't for me, he might have succeeded.'

'Succeeded in killing everyone on Earth, you mean?' Chelsea replied sarcastically. 'Maybe it's not such a bad thing that happened. Would you really rather all of us die?'

'It's not like it won't happen naturally anyway… Just not yet.'

'I can't listen to this, let's go get a drink instead.'

'I dunno if I'm up for it, I-'

'-It's not like you've gotta be up for work in the morning!' Chelsea teased, throwing Ellie's coat at her. 'Get your ass up, we're going out!'

Chapter 13 – The Quirks of Fate

Six weeks later, Ellie's team, now overseen by Hickory, were gearing up to take flight to Calathea.

They had successfully analysed the atmospheric conditions of their destination planet, as well as the propulsion and thrust that would be required to power *Space Shuttle Calathea* across the entire distance.

New technology known as the Inflatable Heat Shield that NASA had been developing for some time to expand and inflate before entering the planet, allowing them to safely land the heavy space shuttle and crew in any atmosphere, including that of Calathea.

A single rover had been designed to act as a vehicle and a Calathean base to house the astronauts during their exhibition on the planet, and high-tech space suits evolved for use everywhere in space, developed using an Exploration Extravehicular Mobility Unit following Artemis Generation Moonwalkers to allow for more natural, Earth like movements, enabling tasks to be completed that were impossible during Apollo missions.

They had only to select the crew that would be embarking on the mission set to take place on 16th July 2022, from Wallops Island Flight Facility.

Despite many recommendations for reinstating Ellie to the mission, having overseen it from the very beginning, Hickory was adamant that she would not be allowed on the premises of the space centre under any circumstances. Instead, Jonny Samson, Emily Sprigg, Edwin Jones and Angelina Frost would be the first men and women to enter Calathea.

On the morning of the launch, two male technicians entered Alexander's glass prison without a word and began to dress him in a specially designed space suit that would restrict his movement, rendering him unable to escape the supervision of the crew.

Having spent over 6 weeks alone in solitary confinement, and many months exposed to the tender mercies of Earth, the concept of returning to his home teased his heart with an overwhelming sense of relief contradicted by a crippling sense of dread.

The launch of the shuttle was broadcast live, worldwide, and for the first time in six weeks Alexander was exposed to the world beyond the four glass walls, and a wealth of people. Hickory, Samson and Jones led him from the isolation unit, through the corridors of the space centre and out into the glorious fresh air and sunshine, while press reporters scrambled to talk to him, shoving microphones in his face and flashing cameras in his eyes.

Under strict instructions to speak to no one, he meandered silently, staring blankly at the ground as he travelled toward the vehicle that would transport him to the flight facility.

After almost 3 hours of travelling, they finally reached the facility.

He was loaded on to the shuttle like cargo, strapped to his seat sandwiched between Samson and Edwin, watching his every move.

A deafening sound filled his ears as he sat inside the circular control centre, white walls surrounded him along with levers, control pads and flashing lights that lit up his pale face decorated with grey bags under his forlorn looking eyes.

'Today is the day, and we have high hopes for our mission. Today, we make history. Today, we revert the crisis looming among mankind and ensure that we can continue to thrive beyond the ozone layer!' William Hickory's voice echoed from several speakers blaring into the crowd of journalists and paparazzi stationed at a safe distance from the shuttle.

Images fluctuating from Hickory's face to the live space shuttle were displayed by a huge screen all across America, streamed by most viewing platforms and watched by millions of fascinated onlookers.

Among the fascinated onlookers, was Ellie, dressed in black with her hood up and her coat zipped all the way up to her chin.

The roar of cheering and applause was drowned by the explosion of flames and smoke pouring from the bottom of *Space Shuttle Calathea* as it prepared for blast off.

A series of painfully beautiful images flickered in Alexander's mind as he ignored the astronauts around him conducting final checks, strapping themselves in and operating the control panel.

Wilbur's cold, wet nose brushing his cheek, the glorious orange sunsets, the forest positively bursting with the most stunning nature and the calm ocean gently lapping at the edge of the shore, tickling his toes.

He was well and truly crushed by the harsh realisation that Calathea as he knew it would be destroyed by the invasion of Earthly humans. He imagined the devastating deforestation, the trusting wildlife being violated by the selfish intentions of the unwelcome intruders. Litter washing up on the white sand, air pollution, destruction...

His mind was whipped into a frenzy as the space shuttle lurched from the ground into the sky at a frightening speed.

That was it.

The sanctuary intended to shield the Omniscients and their fellow inhabitants from humanity was doomed to follow the path of the Earth into chaos and iniquity.

And it was all down to him.

Space Shuttle Calathea soared through the atmosphere until it broke from the Ozone layer and descended into space. The unsettling sound quietened as they exited atmospheric conditions and entered the vacuum of space.

Sprigg, Samson, Jones and Frost each unfastened the belts securing them to their seats, leaving Alexander restrained.

He could but stare emotionlessly out of the glass into the darkness, powerless.

Through glassy eyes, he noticed a flash shooting through the blackness at an impressive speed toward Earth, and a mere few moments later, the crew navigating the space shuttle were frozen in their positions, Sprigg and Frost gazing through the window, while Samson and Jones studied the control panel.

Slightly alarmed, Alexander squirmed in his restrictive space suit in an attempt to free himself...

Meanwhile, Althea, Sebastian and Azriel landed effortlessly on the tarmac beside the silenced journalists and paparazzi, gravely concerned by the enormous empty space they expected to be occupied by the space shuttle.

They were dressed in slim, gold coloured, holographic long sleeve shirts tucked into black trousers and black boots with white laces.

'We're too late.' Azriel said slowly. 'The shuttle has departed.'

Althea blinked frantically as she stared about the flight facility.

'Where is my son, Azriel?' She asked reluctantly, having already drawn a terrifying conclusion.

'Alexander was on the space shuttle.' Azriel answered, unconvinced by the merit of sugar-coating this to his wife.

'You're Alex's parents?' Ellie asked, emerging from the sea of human statues, Alexander's necklace visible through the now open zip of her coat.

'What's that around your neck?' Sebastian asked, pointing to the gift he had bestowed upon the boy many years before.

'This is... his necklace. I haven't seen him to give it back.' She replied cautiously. 'What's going on here?'

'You are Alexander's friend, Ellie. Is that correct?' Azriel inquired.

'That's right.' She smiled awkwardly. 'Which one of you is "Uncle Sebastian"? He said you gave this to him. I guess you should have it back.'

She unhooked the necklace and held it out. As Sebastian took it from her hand, she too became a human statue.

'That *is* a relief. I thought she was some kind of super-human!' Sebastian joked.

Althea and Azriel turned to him, unimpressed.

'This is no time for cracking wise, Sebastian. This is very serious. Before we know it, the space shuttle will be landing on Calathea, the planet we were specifically instructed to keep separate from human influence.' Azriel barked.

'With all due respect, Azriel, standing here patronising me isn't going to help any more than me making a joke.' He handed the necklace back to Ellie, reviving her. 'How long will it take for the space shuttle to reach Calathea, Ellie?'

Ellie narrowed her eyes in thought.

'Given how close the planet is to Earth, I estimate for it to take about 6 hours. We have advanced the technology used to power the shuttles reducing the travel time significantly.'

'How long ago did the shuttle blast off?' Althea responded immediately.

'About… a half hour ago.' Ellie replied, glancing at her phone to confirm the time.

'Do you think we could intercept it?' Althea asked.

'Not without injuring the crew. Including Alex.' Ellie verified.

Althea glanced at Ellie somewhat sternly, hearing her refer to her son as 'Alex'.

'Then, how are we going to stop them from landing on Calathea?' Sebastian interjected.

'We can't.' Althea and Azriel said at the same time.

They stood in silence, panic rising among the group.

As they considered their desperate situation, they noticed the ground begin to tremor gently, increasing in frequency as time crept on.

'We weren't expecting an Earthquake…' Ellie announced suspiciously as the ground shook so violently that she lost her balance and fell.

She looked up to the sky and noticed the grey clouds drifting across the sky an incredible amount faster than she had ever seen.

'Are you guys doing this?' She asked pointing to the sky and glancing across the Omniscients' faces nervously, noticing how easily they were keeping their balance on the trembling floor. 'Ok, this is really starting to freak me out-'

She scrambled to her feet and a sharp jolt knocked her to the floor once more. The clouds whizzed by overhead, graduating to a darker shade of grey with every passing second.

'Is there any technology inside this building that would allow you to investigate the scale of this strange occurrence?' Azriel asked Ellie.

'Uhh… Yeah, I guess, but my key was confiscated, I can't get in.' She responded, looking slightly ashamed.

'Lead on.' He commanded, offering his hand to pull her to her feet.

As instructed, Ellie directed the Omniscients to the entrance of the flight facility, presenting the well-armed glass door, reinforced to repel intruders, such as themselves.

Althea swiped her hand across the proximity reader and a subtle golden glow sank into the technology, igniting a small green light and releasing the lock on the door.

'How did you-'

'Please, there is no time to waste.' Althea interrupted Ellie, who immediately sprung to action, briskly making for the stairs.

The Omniscients followed, until they reached a room filled with people frozen over their desks and staring at the large screen displaying *Space Shuttle Calathea* as it took to the sky.

Shoving a nameless employee out of the way, Ellie took his seat behind his computer and began to explore the system, Sebastian, Althea and Azriel anxiously peering over her shoulder.

Althea noticed the *'ALIENS IN AMERICA?'* newspaper entry strewn across a nearby desk, and was sickened by the very thought that her son was regarded as an outcast. Azriel had not told her of the injuries he sustained at the hands of humanity, but she was sure to find out eventually.

'This isn't an Earthquake.' Ellie began, squinting at her screen through her glasses. 'This is happening everywhere. The Earth's entire crust is experiencing shockwaves. Why this is happening, I can't say...' Her voice trailed anxiously.

A shrill beep began to sound and nearby buildings collapsed as the shaking of the ground grew more violent. The shattering of glass and thud of crumbling concrete drilled through the walls and Ellie began to lose her nerve.

'We've gotta get out of here, guys!' She shrieked as the sea of statues outside were crushed by a neighbouring building clattering to the ground they were fixed to. 'Come on!'

Without a backward glance, she rushed out of the room toward the door through which they had entered the building.

Sebastian, Althea and Azriel dashed after her, and Sebastian snatched Alexander's necklace from her grip. She was left frozen as she lunged for the door handle, an expression of sheer panic plastered across her face.

'Could this be Anad's doing?' Sebastian asked his comrades.

'I strongly suspect so.' Aziel replied immediately. 'He must be aware of the space shuttle departing the Earth.'

'We must leave immediately.' Althea declared firmly. 'Could we possibly locate the space shuttle and divert its path?'

'With Alexander on board?!' Sebastian cried.

'The hysterical girl, perhaps she could be of assistance?' Althea suggested, desperate to retrieve her son, who was trapped in the space shuttle and edging closer to Calathea, with the crew still statues.

A chandelier crashed to the floor dangerously close to where they were stood, and Sebastian crammed the necklace back into Ellie's hand. They darted out of the door and Ellie stumbled across the quivering ground toward the empty space once occupied by *Space Shuttle Calathea*. The Omniscients followed.

The sound of buildings collapsing filled the air and enormous clouds of dust rose in the sky, joining the quickening conveyor belt of now black clouds circling the sky.

'If we can catch the space shuttle, will you be able to gain entry, Ellie?' Althea asked, holding the woman's arm to keep her from falling to the ground.

'Catch? A space shuttle?' Ellie responded sceptically.

'In order for this to work, you need to trust us.' Althea stared sincerely into Ellie's eyes as the Earth began to fall apart around them. 'Can you get us on the shuttle?'

Ellie stared back for a moment.

'Yes.' She finally responded.

Dressed in the space suit that she should have worn when the space shuttle, now 3 hours into its journey, blasted off, Ellie stood opposite the three Omniscients.

Azriel took Althea's hand and Althea took Sebastian's.

They formed a circle around Ellie, and a golden ring shone around the congregation. The ring rose from the ground, lifting Ellie and engulfing the bodies of the Sebastian, Althea and Azriel which fizzled into shadows of shiny dust that surged upwards as Ellie gathered height, powered by the engine of Omniscients.

The flight facility crumbled into a pile of useless rubble as they ascended, along with many other buildings coming crashing down with the hope of Earthly humans ever 'thriving beyond the Ozone Layer', as William Hickory promised they would.

Clouds sliced across Ellie's space suit as they frantically circled the sky. She looked down on the Earth as it crumbled at the power of Anad's influence.

Dizzy, she closed her eyes as she shot out of the atmosphere and into space in hot pursuit of the space shuttle. What she didn't notice, was the clouds catching fire as the Earth veered dangerously close to the sun...

The Earth's crust shuddered ever more violently as the temperature rapidly rose, quickening the convection currents beneath the mantle. Volcanoes erupted, tsunamis roared across coastlines and the air was dark with ash, smoke and dust from the debris of all evidence of humanity.

Meanwhile, aboard the space shuttle, Alexander was becoming increasingly alarmed as the control panels screamed and flashed at the lifeless astronauts that were powerless to attend to it. Tethered to his seat and restrained by the straight jacket of a space suit he was wearing, Alexander was just as powerless.

Ellie felt weightless as she flew through the vacuum of space, strangely comforted by the enormous, empty darkness. It was like she has been relieved of her Earthly burdens and introduced to a life more simple, the life that Alexander described to her that she swore she could never be satisfied with. Her anxieties melted away into the nothingness that surrounded her, and an unfamiliar feeling of content tingled through her very being.

She opened her eyes just as the space shuttle became visible. She was momentarily elated, until her spirits were shaken as she spotted Calathea in the near distance. They could not be more than twenty minutes from entering its atmosphere. She knew they would have to act with all possible speed if they were to influence matters in any way.

They finally caught up with the shuttle, and Ellie gripped the edge of the machine for dear life as she attempted to tease the entry door open. She managed to haul it open just wide enough for her to slip onto the shuttle, and the navigated to the control room where a scene of utter chaos lay.

The quiet of space was disturbed by the deafening sirens squealing from the control panel. The sight of Alexander, his helmet steamed by his obvious panic, his limbs squirming beneath the tight clamps of his seat.

Ellie didn't know which disaster to tend to first. Quickly unfastening his tethers, she failed to engage further with Alexander and turned her attention to the failing systems on the control panel.

A linear flash carved through the air before Alexander's eyes, and a small pop of light flashed to reveal his beloved Omniscient family, of whose company he had been deprived of for many months.

Fearing that they were a figment of his imagination having been driven mad by his weeks of isolation, Alexander could but stare, dumbfounded by the presence of his saviours.

Althea unclasped his helmet and dropped it to the floor, placing a gentle hand on his soft cheek. Her eyes welled with tears as she sensed his broken spirits through the windows to his soul. The emerald eyes that were once full of joy and hope were now dull and despairing. Her heart was crushed beneath her ribs.

The squeal of the alarms silenced, and the space shuttle fast approached Calathea.

'What do you want me to do? Do you want me to land this thing on your planet or shall I try and redirect our course back to Earth?' Ellie shouted, her voice muffled by her helmet.

Unaware of the carnage unfolding on Earth, Azriel instructed her to divert the course of the space shuttle.

She did so, and they collectively breathed a premature sigh of relief.

Chapter 14 – A Leap of Faith

Amused by the sight of the crew trapped inside their own minds now that he was finally set at liberty, Alexander was enormously comforted by the presence of his family, but strangely contradicted by the heavy sense of failure he felt.

'It's over, sweetheart.' Althea said softly, taking Alexander's hand. 'You are safe. And so is Calathea.'

'No thanks to me.' He replied. 'Had you not intervened, humanity would have invaded our sacred haven.'

'We could not have foreseen-'

'-Nonetheless, all is well that ends well, I suppose.' Alexander forced a weak smile and turned to his father, before his expression darkened. 'Concordia, the Omniscient who never returned from Earth...'

Althea and Azriel exchanged nervous looks.

'Did you see her?' Sebastian lunged forward, his eyes desperate and wild, his pounding heart practically visible through his clothing with the impossible prospect of her still being alive. 'Where is she?'

'Uncle Sebastian… She-'

A furious orange flash interrupted Alexander's tragic realisation as the space shuttle approached Earth once more.

The Omniscients turned to see the fantastically terrifying image of Earth spinning like a bowling ball into the gigantic flaming star that is the sun.

As they collided, a truly deafening roar radiated from the impact, and a surge of flames resembling a tidal wave raced toward the space shuttle.

For a moment, everything was frozen.

Every person, every being, every hope, dream and aspiration that once existed on Earth disintegrated into a cosmic dust.

A heavy emptiness descended upon Eleanor Johnson's being as she witnessed the end of the world through her own eyes, from a space shuttle she was not supposed to be on.

The brief lag in time came to an abrupt end and the control panel of the space shuttle began to squeal as the hungry sea of flames swallowed them up.

The angry glare of the fire flashed in Ellie's desperate eyes as she clambered to gain control of the machine.

Althea snatched Alexander's necklace from Ellie, and she froze where she stood.

'We must go!' She cried, grabbing Alexander's hand and attempting to drag him toward the exit of the space shuttle. He stayed rooted, refusing to leave Ellie behind.

The space shuttle groaned as the fire eating away at its structure crumpled the metal.

'I am not leaving her!' Alexander shouted over the noise and chaos, looking terribly disappointed in his mother for suggesting they abandon the very woman that had helped them.

'Alexander-'

'I am *not* leaving her, mother.' He interrupted sternly.

'She is a *human* and she is not welcome in Calathea!' Althea shouted back at him, tugging at his arm.

They stared at one another for a moment, the space shuttle beginning to collapse around them.

Alexander ripped his necklace from his mother's hand and returned it to Ellie's possession, startling her back to life.

'Alex, there's nothing I can do!' She cried. 'This thing is gonna explode any minute!'

'Come with me!' He instructed, taking her hand.

Althea shot her a glare that said 'don't'.

Ellie didn't move.

'What are you doing? We have to go!' Alexander asked frantically.

'You have to go, leave me here.' She said calmly among the chaos.

Alexander screwed up his face, utterly bewildered by what she had just said.

'You were sent on a mission to stop any human from entering the new world. And you did it!' She giggled, tears filling her eyes. 'So leave me here, and make sure nobody in Calathea makes the same mistakes as we did on Earth.'

'I couldn't have done it without you, Ellie!' He squeezed her hands tightly. 'I won't leave you.'

Ellie removed her helmet and threw it to the floor, and planted her lips on Alexander's. The sweat pouring from their faces flickered orange as the flames engulfing the space shuttle grew bigger, wilder, angrier.

'I'll never forget you.' Alexander sobbed as he conceded to her wishes.

Ellie nodded, suffocated by her suppressed hysterics.

Alexander turned to leave, and Sebastian, Azriel and Althea disappeared into space in the direction of Calathea. Before he took his final step, he turned around and grabbed Ellie's hand, only managing a loose grip.

With a tremendous bang, the space shuttle exploded just as Alexander leapt into the vacuum of space.

He felt Ellie's skin brush his hand and tightened his grip to find his fingernails digging into his own flesh.

His heart stopped beating but before he could scan the area to locate Ellie, he transformed into a flash of golden light and soared toward Calathea.

He landed hard on the white sand, his vision blurred, his head spinning, gasping for breath.

Wilbur noticed him immediately and raced across the sand as fast as his legs would carry him to greet his friend. He leapt into his arms and squealed with glee as Alexander embraced him.

He staggered to his feet, holding Wilbur tightly.

'Where is she?' He spluttered.

Where is she?

Appendix

Sources and Definitions:

Omniscient – knowing everything

Calathea – a plant symbolic of new beginnings

Althea (Omniscient of Compromise)– a name of Greek origin, meaning healer/wholesome

Azriel (Omniscient of Unity)– 'one of the four Archangels'

Concordia (Omniscient of Empathy) – a name meaning peace and harmony

Sebastian (Omniscient of Abundance) – means 'venerable' or 'revered' in Latin

Anad (Omniscient Commander) – a Zoroastrian name meaning 'elements of God'

Prima (Omniscient Commander) – a name of Latin origin meaning 'first'

Pandora (Mistress of the herd) – a name meaning 'all-giving'

Potenza (Master of the herd) – a name meaning power and strength

Phoenix (Pandora and Potenza's son) – a name meaning resurrection

Gerda Weissmann Klein –

A real survivor of the Holocaust who sadly passed away in April 2022.

Information regarding Gerda's experience as told by herself was obtained from a video shared by 'RISE by Goalcast' across social media. The chapter in which she features is a transcription of the video consisting entirely of her own words and those of her husband.

NASA –

Much of the information regarding new technologies being developed by NASA was extorted directly from NASA's website: https://science.nasa.gov/earth-science

Though the information is relatively accurate, there are elements that have been tweaked for the convenience of the fictional storyline, for example; the timeline for building a space shuttle has been reduced in the story.

Ingram Content Group UK Ltd.
Milton Keynes UK
UKHW021819160523
421856UK00010B/199